GRAVE MISGIVINGS

ROCK HIS WORLD
BOOK THREE

EVIE RILEY

Grave Misgivings
Rock His World
Book Three
Copyright © 2025 Evie Riley
ISBN: 978-1-77357-743-2
978-1-77357-744-9
Published by Naughty Nights Press LLC
Cover Art By Willsin Rowe

CHAPTER 1

GEO

"Just a little to the left," Kevin, my manager, directs.

I shift my weight, turning my torso slightly to the left, and the camera flashes.

"No, no. I mean your whole body, Geo. I want you to pull that arm back, show off those fucking muscles and abs you work so hard for."

I roll my eyes, biting my tongue as I do what he says, even though it pisses me off.

But then again, photo shoots *always* piss me off. Everyone's so demanding and brutal in how they talk to you, let alone how they pose you.

You think after ten years, I'd be used to this. But every time it's like a fresh hell.

I shouldn't have to show my abs to sell records.

I didn't need abs when I was part of the Christian Rock circuit.

I shove the thought away, because I know that only leads me to depression. Any time I think about how things *used* to be before I signed with Casualty Records usually puts me in a funk.

And the last thing I want is to look as pissy as I feel for these promo images Casualty *demanded* I get for the upcoming *Pillars Of Rock* Tour.

Seriously, even Mateo and Felix don't have to endure this as much as I do.

Probably because they are walking wet dreams, and I'm a fucking forty-year-old virgin. God save me.

Okay, well, I'm not forty *yet,* but close enough. My damn birthday is about a month and a half away, and I'll actually be home in Arizona to perform and to celebrate with my family during the tour.

Though I can't say I'm thrilled to be going home, either, because I know that's a clusterfuck waiting to happen too. Because I'll be near *him.*

My former bandmate, Zebulon Ingram, aka Zeb, is one of those things in life that I am convinced exists to remind me that nothing can be perfect.

That I am not without sin, and I am not without consequence.

Leaving home to pursue this record deal was everything I'd prayed for. For myself, and for us as a band, even though, technically, he was just my guitarist.

But Zeb didn't *want* the fame and fortune, the bright shiny lights.

And he didn't want to *change* himself.

As far as I was concerned, my image was a fair trade for the fame and fortune. If Casualty wanted to transform me like Katniss in the *Hunger Games* from a scrawny, nerdy Christian boy next door into a dark, sculpted, tattooed rockstar, I was more than game. This was my *dream.*

Playing sold out shows, hearing my song on the radio, and experiencing the world on a grander scale than Posdosh, Arizona could ever offer me.

My family thought I was selling my soul to the literal devil, and maybe they were right.

The devil is in the details, after all, and the details are what keep my checks coming in, what keeps me on the label despite my floundering sales as of late.

"Okay, better, but can you lean back a little more and grab your cock?"

I shoot Kevin a look of disdain, gaping at him. "Absolutely not!" I bark, feeling a fresh bout of anger and embarrassment.

Kevin only shrugs. "It was worth a shot," he replies as the cameras flash.

"Highly inappropriate," I respond, feeling flustered.

I'm not stupid, I know sex sells, but I also know that part of that has to do with confidence. Confidence I don't fucking have, because sex is very much removed from my life. That whole fake it 'til you make it thing... yeah, I am not good at *that*—the being sexy thing—at all.

At first, the label ran with it. Tried to play up the whole purity ring angle when they discovered I had one, while always showcasing me shirtless in promo and featuring me on all the talk shows to talk about it. Which was probably cute and attractive when I was twenty-nine, but now...

Now it's just a whisper, and it's not a *good* whisper.

How am I supposed to feel when everyone around me thinks I'm a fucking joke?

How is that supposed to make anyone feel confident and sexy?

I prop my leg out, swing my arm back so my leather jacket rises back enough to show the cut of my well-defined hipbones.

I guess the lack of a sex life is a win for the damn gym. It certainly helps take the edge off, most days.

I focus my gaze on the camera, channeling my best impression of Mateo Starr, the lead singer of *Mage Of Mercy* and the closest thing I have to a best friend nowadays since Zeb and I haven't spoken in ten years.

Mateo is the most commanding, confident motherfucker I know, so it usually helps if I try to impersonate someone I *know* is sexy and can command attention.

"Oh, baby, that is *fire!*" Kevin says as the cameras flash. "Look at that fucking v! Delicious."

His praise doesn't feel as good as it should.

Because this—clad in leather, showing off my muscles and making sex eyes at the camera—isn't really me. Not by a long shot.

I don't know who decided looking constipated and being dressed like a German fetishist was "hot", but one day I'd like to have a word with them.

"Are we done?" I ask as the flashing stops.

"Yeah, I think we got some decent shots. You can wrap it up."

I sigh in relief. I slide off my jacket, reaching for my tank top. My phone buzzes in my back pocket and I grab it once I'm dressed.

I see a couple texts. One from my sister begging me to call her, and one from Hailee Starr, the other half of *Mage Of Mercy*.

Celina, Hans, me and Mateo are going out for drinks. You free?

The invite isn't what surprises me, but the fact Mateo is coming, does.

He's been a bit sullen since his relationship with his actor ex took a turn for the worst. I don't know the details, except for the fact that the man cheated on him, though I think there's more to it than what Mateo wants to admit, and I won't press him for it. If Mateo wants to take confession with me, that's fine, but until then, I'm perfectly content to just have a few drinks with the guy and support him however he needs.

I text Hailee back with a thumbs up and she texts me the address and time, which makes me feel a little better.

Kevin claps me on the back. "You know I'm not trying to be a pain in your ass, right?" he says, imploring me with his deep brown eyes.

I'm comfortable enough in my own skin to admit Kevin's an attractive guy, which is also why I don't think he gets my resistance.

The man has probably never felt inadequate in his life, and I doubt he has a problem finding a girlfriend. Or boyfriend. Or something.

I've tried to date, really I have. But every woman I am interested in seems to think she's going to be the one to taint my innocence or some shit, and then they're downright pissed when I pump the brakes or tell them I don't want to rush things.

What is wrong with wanting to get to know someone before the sex stuff?

What is wrong with wanting to fucking wait for the *right* person?

I brush Kevin's hand off my shoulder, knowing he's not *trying* to be a dick.

"I'd like to see *you* get in front of a camera and have a hundred pairs of eyes watching you. Telling you to grab your cock like you're a piece of meat."

Kevin sighs. "We've talked about this, Geo. The label wants—"

"I know what the label wants," I snap. "But what about what I want, Kev?" I head for the exit.

"What do you want, Geo? Some water, some chips, some—"

"No, Kevin. A bag of Takis isn't going to make me feel spicy."

"I don't get it, man, you act like you're *not* fucking two time grammy winner *Gravedigger*, man. Seriously, you act like you're some nerd trapped in a rockstar's body or something."

I shoot him a scathing look. "The fact you don't understand that I *am* both astounds me."

"God, you are fucking pissy today," he says.

"Yeah, having people yell at you and telling you to act like a damn stripper will do that to a person."

"It's just a picture, Geo, Christ. It's not like

I'm asking you to open an Only Fans or something."

I sigh, knowing this argument isn't going to get either of us anywhere. Kevin will never understand.

My text goes off, and it's Jinger.

How was the shoot today, cutie?

I sigh, figuring the starlet at the center of Casualty Records is as good a distraction as any.

"I'll see you tomorrow, Kevin." I wave him off as I stroll through the door.

"Bright and early!" he calls out after me.

I slowly amble my way through the hallway to my Camaro. Most of the guys on the label have fancy as shit cars, me included. Goes along with the "image" Casualty wants me to uphold. Though I prefer taking the Lexus, I try to at least take out the flashy one every now and then to try and help myself remember what I've accomplished.

You know, the usual. I text her back.

I lean against my car, watching the bubbles pop up as I wait for her reply.

Jinger is one of those personalities that you either love, or you hate.

The fact she's probably slept with most of

the guys on the label at one point or another—save for Felix, Mateo, and the new kids on the label, *Heart Killer*—usually sets people off. But to be honest, that's why I like Jinger.

Because she doesn't give a shit what people think or say about her. She just does what she wants, and I think that's admirable.

I bet you killed it as always! Her enthusiasm is kind of endearing even if it's drenched in flirtation.

But I don't take her flirting to heart. Jinger flirts with everyone. She's like the human equivalent of a margarita meets Bubbles from the PowerPuff Girls.

Yeah, well, hopefully this satisfies the label, because I'm over this whole "Sexy Geo" thing the label keeps shoving down my throat.

Jinger texts back almost instantly. *I think you're plenty sexy, Geo.*

I run a hand through my hair as her words settle on me. It's not like it's the first time Jinger's said as much. She tells me all the time, like if she says it enough I'll believe her.

Thanks, but I think we both know who's the sexy starlet here, J.

It's true. While I may at least have my big

cross tattoo and a sculpted body, my face isn't quite on par with the rest of me. I can barely grow a fucking beard at thirty-nine, which is embarrassing as fuck.

But Jinger is the total package, a full on knockout who's probably plastered all over teenage bedrooms across the nation. But I've never felt attracted to Jinger in *that* way. Still, you'd have to be blind not to know she's hot as hell.

I run a hand over my face, feeling like an absolute grump.

I'm sorry, I'm just in a funk today, J.

Jinger sends me back a 'k' text, and that's that.

I stare at the black shimmer of my Camaro, my reflection glinting in the sun.

My image stands out, my dark hair blowing in the wind.

I can see the faint ink through my white tank top, the definition in my arms.

It's me, but it isn't.

In so many ways, I feel like I'm still the same awkward guy I was over a decade ago; before the tattoo, before the body, before the fame.

I sigh in exasperation.

With the way I feel right now, maybe a night out with my friends is exactly what I need to get out of this mood.

Because for the first time in ten years, as I look at myself, I don't know the man looking back at me.

CHAPTER 2

GEO

I swallow harshly as I look up at the sign for Saint & Sinner, the *sex* club Mateo agreed to get us into.

I wasn't expecting the night to go this way, to be honest, but after *Heart Killer*'s main frontmen, brothers Dare and Richie Wylde, showed up at the damn restaurant and hijacked the evening, I found myself intrigued.

I've been to a few clubs over the years, usually on dates, but those clubs were usually standard bars and dance floors. I've never been to a strip club or a sex club before, but I didn't want to be the odd man out, especially because Mateo *never* wants to go... well, anywhere.

So, the fact he'd agreed to get us all into the newest hot spot in LA was kind of a big deal, and I wanted to support my friend emerging back into the world.

But I was not prepared for *this*.

I don't have much time to rethink things, because as soon as I *do* consider turning around, Hailee and Richie show up.

Hailee casts me a sly smile, her eyes alight with excitement.

"This is going to be a blast!" she gushes, her smile warming my nerves, if only a fraction.

"It's going to be something, that's for sure," I say as I note Celina and Hans bounding over to us, followed by a stoic Mateo and the younger Wylde brother, Dare.

I don't miss the way Mateo casually slides his hands in his pockets, pretending not to look at the other man, and that alone makes me forget about my own insecurities.

I'm not here for *me*. I'm here for my friend, and that's enough to push away my feelings for the moment.

Mateo does his magic, speaking to the man at the front of the ropes, bypassing the gigantic line. Cameras flash, and fans holler around us. Within seconds, Mateo is waving us all in, and I make my way through the warm LA night, stopping to take a few selfies and sign a few boobs.

When I finally make my way into the club, I can't help but marvel at the sight.

Once I come through a long, dark tunnel, I'm let out in a room that can only be described as the most stylized version of heaven I think I've ever seen.

The stage is lit up with ice-like plexiglass, and there are strippers on the stage, dancing and climbing their silver and white poles.

I casually walk past the main stage, noticing the strippers dressed in white, feathery lingerie. My gaze travels up their long, toned legs, appreciating the physicality of how they move. How they grip the pole with their thighs, flip, and climb the damn thing like it's the monkey bars on a playground and not a damn stripper pole.

They're pretty, but I don't see the appeal, though I can appreciate the athleticism in their moves. I know that's got to take some core strength.

Then again, I've never really found women's lingerie to be that intriguing, mostly because I don't understand the purpose.

Why dress up in tiny pieces of clothing that don't cover you?

If the point is to be naked, why not just be naked?

Then again, I guess I'm not the best judge of seduction, so what the fuck do I know?

I've never seduced *anyone* in my life, and if I tried, I'm sure I'd come off like Steve Carrel getting his fucking chest waxed.

"You okay?" Mateo's voice pulls me from my thoughts and I turn around, nearly knocking him over. I'd only had one drink at the restaurant, so I can't even blame my jumpiness on the alcohol.

I glance around the room, taking in the sight of the sparkling bar, the bright, airy lights and the blue neon.

It's like Antarctica meets the pearly gates.

Another stripper attendant waltzes past me, casting me a sexy smile that barely registers on my radar.

"Yeah, I'm good, why?" I feign nonchalance.

Mateo smirks at me, nudging my shoulder.

"You look like you've entered the seventh circle of Hell."

I sigh, letting out a dry laugh. "I mean, it's just... a lot."

Dare passes us, and I raise an eyebrow at him, a smirk playing on my lips as he casually leads me to what I assume is our VIP booth for the night. Celina, Hans, Richie, Hailee are scattered about, some with drinks in hand already.

I shrug as a woman in an angel outfit—because dress would indicate there was actual fabric to cover things—and a man in tight, white shorts with wings come to our booth, dropping off a large tray of fruits, juices, and two bottles of champagne.

"Compliments of management," the woman says, batting her eyelashes at me.

I nod as Hailee squeals with excitement.

The woman doesn't drop her gaze, almost as if she is waiting for me to say something.

Mateo nods at her. "Thank you. That'll be all for now." His voice is back to that commanding, authoritative tone I know well.

The woman drops her gaze, and for the moment, I am thankful Mateo knows just how to control a room. As well as the people in it, naturally.

Another talent I *wish* I possessed.

The cute angel boy glances at me from under his lashes, chewing on his lips.

"If you need anything, my name's Rex." His voice is drenched in a southern drawl that is as rich as dark chocolate.

His golden blond hair falls in his ocean blue eyes, and I can't help but feel a bit warm. Likely, because I'm practically melding together with Mateo from this angle while Celina, Hans, Hailee, and Richie set about to pouring drinks and snapping selfies.

"Thanks, but I think we're good," I reply, swallowing harshly.

Maybe Mateo's right, maybe I need a drink.

Or two.

Or three.

Something to take the edge off and make me feel like the rockstar everyone keeps telling me I am.

Something to make me think about anything except Rex's thick drawl and cerulean gaze.

I mean, you'd have to be an idiot not *to notice he's built like a damn brick house.*

So he's good looking.

So what?

So are the other strippers. They're probably all models.

Rex slides past me, knocking into my shoulder, forcing me to catch his dark gaze.

"I love your music, by the way," he says, that sweet drawl warm on my skin as he leans close to me. "*Devil In Me* and *Heaven Sent* are totally on my fuck me playlist."

I swallow harshly again, my gaze dipping to his lips.

Yeah, I definitely need a drink.

"Thanks," I manage to say, my voice slightly rough.

He smiles as he walks away.

"Champagne?" Hailee offers me a glass, grinning.

"Absolutely," I agree as I grab the flute from her hand.

Richie calls a toast, and we all clink our glasses, cheering Mateo and the upcoming *Pillars Of Rock* tour.

Hailee smirks at me. "*Heaven Sent* is a great song, you know," she says sweetly. "And that bass line in *Devil In Me* is—" She whistles and I blush.

I down my champagne like it's a shot, relishing in the taste of the fizzy sweetness, reaching for the bottle to pour another glass.

Mateo watches me out of the corner of his eye, but he doesn't say anything.

I try my best to change the subject.

"It's so..." I swallow harshly, taking in the sight of everything, feeling slightly overwhelmed.

Mateo nonchalantly shifts a little closer to me, but not in an overbearing way.

Mateo has always had like this sixth sense of just knowing when something is going on, or if you are having an existential crisis, like I am, at the moment. His gray-blue eyes implore me.

"Relaxing?" he taunts, elbowing me, much in the way an older brother would. Technically, he *is* older than me.

By a couple weeks, but still.

"I was going to say... bright," I tout, crossing my arms as another waitress in a white and blue angel uniform squeezes past us, clearly headed for the table beside us.

"Oh, that's just Saint's aesthetic. The dungeons are downstairs. Where the real sinners go," Mateo annoys me, raising his eyebrows.

I roll my eyes, taking another pull of my champagne.

Kill me now.

Why did I agree to this?

Mateo doesn't talk about his... preferences, but he had called me when shit went sour with his ex, Edward. I don't know the steamy details of what happened, or how their relationship worked in general, but just because I'm a fucking virgin doesn't mean I don't know about the kind of debauchery that is a permanent fixture in Hollywood.

I know Mateo is into some kinky BDSM shit, even if he hasn't been as direct about it, and honestly, I'd be surprised if he *wasn't*.

Some guys just have that vibe, you know?

Like, they exude sex appeal and part of that appeal comes from the fact that they *know* shit. Not just how to command a room, but...

They know how to make you see fucking stars when you come.

I mean, I wouldn't know. But I've heard stuff.

He grins, letting out a laugh as I flip him off. He takes it stride, though.

"And the Hell aesthetic is stereotypically black and red."

"Of course it is," I murmur as Hailee and Celina squeal with excitement, dragging Richie and Hans to the dance floor.

"Dungeons? Like Dungeons and Dragons?" Dare speaks up inquisitively, drawing my attention to his curious gaze.

Mateo turns to him as well, and I don't miss the way he raises his eyebrow at the young twenty-something man.

Dare's expression is like a babe in the woods. I would have assumed someone like him— young, attractive, with boatloads of charisma— would be more than familiar with a place like this.

I mean, isn't that what young twenty-something guys do?

Go to clubs?

Fuck bitches, get money, and all that?

I mean, I wouldn't know, because my twenties were spent at religious fairs and conservative events, and I had a fucking curfew. Try dating in your twenties with a fucking chaperone and a curfew.

Tiffany, my first serious girlfriend came when

I was twenty-one, and my manager—my mother, at the time—had a fucking field day with it.

That's why I always liked working with Zeb, to be honest. I didn't have to pretend to be someone I wasn't with him. Despite my fucked up image and lack of a love life, Zeb didn't care what I did or didn't know about anything, and it was the one place I could escape being *Geo Graves*, Christian Rock Artist, and just be... me. For a couple years, anyway.

It was always about the music and nothing more.

Zeb was a safe place, despite the fact he's the same age as my sister.

What did that say about me?

That at twenty-six, my best friend was a damn sixteen-year old?

A sixteen-year old who was a musical genius, but still.

"You've got to be kidding me," Mateo drawls as I attempt to pour myself another glass of champagne, if only because I don't want to think about how terrible of an idea this was.

"What are you even still doing here? Aren't you supposed to be out there?" Mateo's voice pulls me from my brooding walk down memory lane, and I turn to see him motion to Dare, shooing him and insinuating he should leave.

His tone is bitter, sarcastic, but I don't miss the way his entire body shifts, or the way he adjusts his damn jeans. Nonchalantly, of course.

I shoot Mateo a bombastic side-eye, because even though I *know* Dare didn't notice, I'm more than sure it wasn't coincidental.

I clutch my drink, and Mateo shrugs me off, proverbially flipping me an invisible finger as if to say, "You didn't see shit, G."

I've never had any issue with the fact Mateo is openly gay, despite the fact I was raised in purity culture. Actually, if I'm being honest, it's always been kind of a blessing because it is a lot easier *knowing* he is, because like Zeb, I don't have to worry about sex the way I do when I am with everyone who is straight. And I never assumed just because Mateo was gay that he was into me, like so many men do.

As if being a man in the presence of a man who likes men is an automatic *I want to fuck you*.

Besides, I'm not his type, and even if I was, it still wouldn't bother me, I don't think.

Mateo has always been cool with the fact I've built my career on being a virgin and straight edge, and I've always been cool with the fact that he was openly gay and a bit of a dick to everyone but the people he truly cares about.

I feign a look away, but I'd be lying if I said I wasn't interested in the rare mating event happening before my eyes. Seriously, it is like watching a National Geographic Special on Caveman Rituals.

Because honestly, it doesn't make any sense. Mateo, the poised, sarcastic, dark and moody sexpot, and the cute, young, emo golden retriever.

"What about you? You just going to sit here all night like a Kingpin?" Dare bites back at Mateo, who regards him with an annoyed look.

"I do not engage," Mateo replies.

It feels like I'm watching something I have no business watching, but like a train wreck, I can't look away, either.

Something about their exchange and banter makes me homesick.

For something I haven't thought about in years.

"You like to watch, is that it?" Dare raises an eyebrow at Mateo as he goes for a glass of champagne, tossing a handful of strawberries in his glass, which makes some of the liquid spill out of the sides.

"What I like is none of your fucking business. Besides, you are stalling." Mateo huffs, his tone flustered and on edge.

I can't help the smirk that forms on my lips.

Mateo Starr isn't so easily rattled, and the fact Dare can get under his skin so easily makes me like the kid all the more.

"Stalling for what?" My gaze drifts to Rex, who shoots me a sly grin as he drops off another bottle of champagne and a fresh bowl of strawberries.

Thankfully, Mateo speaks before I have to awkwardly thank the angel who keeps staring at me like *I'm* the bowl of strawberries. It makes me uncomfortable.

Who the fuck am I kidding, this whole place makes me uncomfortable because I have no clue what I'm fucking doing. Or what I'm supposed *to be doing.*

Dare downs some of his drink, about half in one gulp, before he refills his glass.

I never got to do the whole drinking 'til dawn in my early twenties stage.

I was touring locally with a bunch of other

up and coming Christian Rock groups at the time, dating Tiffany, and curfew was strictly enforced.

But I guess, when in Rome...

"Our darling little *Heart Killer* has a mission tonight." Mateo grins, Dare stopping mid-pour.

"What's that?" I ask, Rex nudging my shoulder as he leaves. The motion puts his skin against mine, and a flush heats my entire body.

His skin is warm, slick with oil, and my damn cock twitches.

I take a heavy sip of my drink, hoping it will make me forget about this entire, weird night and my stupid cock.

Mateo's voice is direct, but it isn't venomous. "Find someone to fuck."

Dare curses and I nearly spit out my champagne. Mateo is always direct, but his words coupled with the attractive man in angelic booty-shorts and wings slithering past me, my buzz, and my cock acting weird as fuck, I can't help myself.

You're just having an off night, G. It's fine. You're fine.

Mateo slaps me on the back, running his hand between my shoulders in a friendly way as he lets out a dark chuckle.

"And what about you, Matty? You take a vow of celibacy I don't know about?" Dare bites back petulantly.

"No," Mateo snaps, and I let out an exasperated breath.

The tension is so thick, and I'm half-concerned the two of them are going to whip out their dicks and have a measuring contest right fucking here.

Like there can only be one Highlander, Dare and Mateo look like they are ready to fight to the death.

Over what I'm not sure, but I know enough of my friend to know the way his jaw is set, he's not as pissed as he looks.

Agitated, maybe, but not pissed.

And all at once, I realize, they aren't dick measuring.

Like pretty peacocks, they're fanning their fucking feathers and trying to *impress* one another. They're flirting.

"Maybe *you* should engage for once. Put yourself back out there," I say, a slow smile forming on my face.

Dare's wide grin spreads and before Mateo can even speak, he *grabs* him, yanking him up from the couch with ease like the man isn't made of solid muscle.

I watch as Dare drags him to the dance floor, watch as my notoriously secluded friend navigates his way through a crowd, and I feel a pang of jealousy.

I watch all of them on the dance floor. Richie and Hailee, Celina and Hans, and Dare and Mateo.

I wish I had *that*.

Confidence, zest. A peacock of my own to pull through the crowd.

I pull out my phone, feeling melancholy alone in the booth with the champagne and an overabundance of fruit.

I fill my glass, noting that I'm starting to feel a little more than buzzed.

Maybe getting drunk is the answer to all my problems.

Likely, not, but I wouldn't know because I've never really *let* myself have more than one or two drinks before, if only because it has been drilled into me from a young age that I need to be a *good boy* and good boys don't stay out past curfew, have sex, or drink in excess.

I know I'm not a kid anymore. I'm fucking

thirty-nine. But some things aren't that easy to let go of.

I scroll through my phone, browsing my contact list, or lack thereof.

Seriously, how sad is it that I barely have thirty people in my phone?

I reach for a strawberry, hoping the fruit quells my brooding.

But it doesn't.

I'm just about to drain the last of my drink and call it a night, when my thumb accidentally hits the call button.

I fumble with my phone, realizing my error, but because of the alcohol, my fingers don't work as fast as they normally do, and the unfortunate soul answers me before I can hang up.

"Hello?" The voice on the other end of the phone makes my heart stop.

It's familiar, in a sense, but it's also foreign.

Deeper, older.

Gravelly.

Like I woke him up or something.

I sit there for a moment, frozen in Saint & Sinner as angels surround me in various states of skimpy outfits, the haze of the blue lights reflecting on my phone.

"Hello?" he says again. "Geo, is that you?"

My breath catches in my throat, and I can barely process his voice.

There are a thousand things I want to say. A thousand stories, a thousand apologies.

But all I manage to say is, "I miss you."

Silence fills the air, and I think I've lost him.

Again.

CHAPTER 3

Zeb

It's near two-thirty in the morning when my phone rings. I answer it without thinking, because I immediately jump to the worst case scenario. Nothing good ever comes from a call at two-thirty am. It's either a booty call or an emergency, and I haven't even fucked anyone in over a year, so I'm pretty sure I've been erased as a booty call from anyone's contacts.

"Hello?" I answered, expecting to hear a familiar voice on the other end of the phone, like Katy.

But all I hear is heavy breathing.

I roll over in my bed, wiping my eyes. If this is some asshole's idea of a prank call...

"Hello?" I try again, thinking maybe, just *maybe*, it's a wrong number, or a butt dial, or—

I pull the phone away from my ear, glancing at the name in the dark, my entire body going numb as I read the caller ID.

Geo.

The heavy breathing sounds louder, and in the distance I hear music. Heavy bass and thumping accompanying what sounds like Ava Max in the background.

I swallow harshly as I roll over on my side, phone clutched to my ear like it is a goddamn lifeline.

It's been ten years.

Ten fucking years.

I'd thought about this day. Fantasized about it even, especially in those early days after he left for L.A.

I used to sit in my bedroom with my acoustic guitar, pouring out my heart into my journal or my sketchbook, and fantasize that he'd call me, out of the blue, and tell me he couldn't do this thing—the band, Hollywood, everything—without me.

That he was coming home to *me*.

But even then, I knew it was nothing more than a fantasy. Because Geo Graves was meant for bigger things than Posdosh, Arizona, and even if he wasn't...

He wasn't *gay*, like me.

After a year, I gave up pining and hoping he'd come to his senses and come back home. And after my twenty-first birthday, I'd decided it was time I put myself out there and move on. From Geo Graves, from wanting a man who had no clue how I really felt about him.

Somehow, I managed to rise from the wreckage Geo left in his wake and I built myself a damn good life over the last ten years.

On my own.

Without *him*.

I'm successful, I have a decent following for my music, I've got my own fucking house, and I've got friends.

Okay, so it's mainly Geo's sister, Katy, but still.

Yet everything I'd worked so hard for, everything I thought I was, flew out the fucking window at two-thirty in the morning the moment I heard his voice.

"Geo, is that you?" I ask, holding onto the

last shred of hope that this is some fucked up prank call, or an accident of some sort.

That I am *imagining* his deep breathing on the other end of the phone because it is fucking two-thirty, and I am alone.

And when I am alone, my thoughts often stray to Geo Graves, even though I don't want them to.

Silence, and another heavy breath.

He sounds drunk.

I close my eyes, realization striking me. He probably has no idea he's called *me*.

I shake my head, knowing it's probably best to just hang up.

To preserve my own dignity, and his.

"I miss you." His voice is sad, guilty.

And very, very drunk.

Maybe he wasn't actually trying to call *me*, maybe he was trying to call...

"Zeb, say something," he pleads.

Ten years.

Ten fucking years, and I feel like I'm sixteen again, waiting, wishing for something, for someone I know I can't have.

And just like before, I cave.

Because I can't stand to hear him like this.

"I miss you too, G," I reply, the words heavy in the air. Even sober, I don't think he'd understand that the way I *miss* him is not the same way he misses me.

"Where are you?" I ask, both wanting to know and also not wanting to know because I know the details will probably only hurt me.

Because they always do.

The loud bass changes to something high tempo, but I can't make out what it is.

Geo sighs, and the sound is deep, dark.

Sexy.

I sit up in my bed, the only light the moonlight shining through my window onto the center of my bed. I swing my arms around my knees, pulling them tight to my chest.

"Sssaint & Sinner," he slurs. "The boy angels are kind of hot. Tight shorts, pretttty wings. Bet the devils are hotter, though."

I don't want to take his bait.

I know he doesn't mean it the way it sounds, but fuck.

If I believed in Heaven and Hell, Geo Graves would be my own personal devil. Tempting me, luring me into a dark pit I'd never want to leave.

"They always are," I say with a slight smirk,

even though I know he can't see me. Part of me wishes he could, though.

I glance at my reflection in the mirror across from my bed, noticing the way my shadowed form takes up space. More space than I used to, that's for sure.

What would he think of the way I've changed?

Would he even recognize me?

I'm certainly not the same person I was at nineteen when he left.

I cross my arms, letting my fingers rove over my thick arms. Nineteen year old me had no muscle at all, but at least I didn't gain ten pounds every time I looked at a damn cheeseburger.

"I missss you," he says again, his voice deep and sexy, then shifting gears, he sighs.

"Is this what sin feels like, Zeb?" He lets out a deep breath. His voice is some mix of sadness and wistfulness, edged with drunken frankness.

I can't find it in my heart to answer him.

Because I don't believe in sin.

But if I did, he would be mine.

I'm pretty sure lusting after your straight friend counts as a sin in someone's book. And if it doesn't, lusting after your best friend's straight brother who's ten years older than you, most definitely does.

"Are you alone?" I asked, unsure if I really want to know the truth.

"I'm always alone," he says, his voice barely a whisper.

"Geo..." I pinch the bridge of my nose. "You're drunk." I say the words for myself, mostly.

Because I can't let myself fall back into old habits.

I can't let him open up the wound I fought so fucking hard to stitch back together.

"Don't tell my mother," he whispers. Then, he laughs.

It's infectious, but then everything about Geo Graves is infectious.

His smile, his spicy orange blossom and clover scent, his pretty fucking eyes and perfect mouth.

His voice.

Oh, that *voice.*

"Secret's safe with me, G." I glance at the clock. It's three am.

We've been talking for a half hour.

And it barely feels like five minutes.

Then I hear voices. Voices I don't recognize.

"We're heading out," a female says. "

You good? You need a ride?" I hear a man's voice, he sounds young.

"Yeah, I think I'm drunk," he says innocently.

The woman chuckles. "That you are, Geo. Come on, let's get you home."

"Home's in Arizonnnna…" he whines, and then I hear some buttons beeping.

I know then he's forgotten about me, about his momentary lapse in judgment.

"Go home, Geo," I say, not waiting for him to respond. I hang up, tossing my phone on the bed as I run my hands through my hair.

I force myself to lie back down, to close my eyes, but it's no use.

I've been poisoned again, and all I can think about is his deep, guilty voice.

I miss you.

Maybe Hell is real after all.

CHAPTER 4

G EO

H AILEE AND R ICHIE giggle as I fumble with my fingers trying to open my digital lock.

"I'm sorry," I say, feeling the need to apologize for my behavior.

Hailee giggles as I lean against her.

"It's okay, Geo. You're allowed to have fun once in a while, you know."

"What's your code?" Richie's voice is slightly raspy, and I know I'm not the only one who had fun tonight.

I tell him, and soon enough the door opens and Hailee helps me through the door.

"Thanks, Hailee," I say, feeling the peak of my life's choices this evening.

She rubs my shoulders. "Of course. You know we got your back." She flashes me with a sweet smile. Her eyes are glassy, too, and I wonder how Mateo and Dare are faring. I never even got to say goodbye.

"See you at the studio," she says as she backs out the door, and when it closes, the resounding click echoes in my foyer.

I stand there, in front of my grand staircase, inexplicably aware of how quiet it is here.

Moments ago, there was noise. Giggling, beeping, curse words, Hailee's excitable voice.

And now there's just nothing.

You think loneliness gets easier, but it doesn't.

It just gets louder when there is no noise to drown out the truth.

I run my hand over my face, knowing I need to shower and go to bed. Chances are, I'll probably feel like shit in the morning, and I'll be less likely to want to do it then.

I climb my steps, the gold and crystal accouterments of my big chandelier refracting off the beige walls like glitter.

The air is cool, and I can't help but think of the temperature in the club.

All those bodies, all that sweat.

All that heat.

I saunter down the hallway, past my framed awards and photos. Those first couple years on the label, I was doing pretty well. Riding the whole purity ring wave didn't hurt our sales then. My cover of Real Life's *Send Me An Angel* went platinum. Twice.

It put me on the map. I was no longer known as the nerdy Christian emo kid, Geo Graves.

I was *Gravedigger.*

I shed my thick glasses, got some contacts, bulked up, dyed my hair, got a big ass tattoo, and flaunted my little silver ring while showing off my abs, and suddenly, I was a hit.

For a little while, anyway.

I head for my bedroom, removing my clothes as I go.

At least on the plus side, being alone means I can technically walk around my house in my birthday suit if I want, pretty much whenever I want.

I traipse across the white marble floor of my

bedroom to my en-suite bathroom, taking stock of myself in the oversized vanity mirror.

I stop for a moment, taking it all in. How much I've changed.

I'm still paler than Vlad The Impaler, but the giant black cross that spans across my entire chest and torso only draws attention to my expertly sculpted hip bones, that wicked "V" that looks like a neon sign, pointing right to my damn dick.

In my black, tight boxer briefs, the contrast is more noticeable.

As is is the outline of my fucking cock.

I chew my bottom lips, my glassy eyes staring back at me as I turn to the side like Kevin told me to at the photoshoot.

These briefs are my favorite, because they have that comfy ball sac thing that feels like fucking heaven, but I guess I never noticed that it makes me look thicker. Bigger.

I slide my tongue over my lips, channeling my best Mateo Starr impression.

Stoic, serious. Sexy.

I cant my neck a little bit as I lean back, sliding my hand over my pronounced, sheathed cock.

My cock twitches from the touch alone, and I have to bite my lip.

I think about Kevin's words, his instructions.

I grab my cock, opening my mouth just the slightest.

"Is that sexy?" I ask myself, but the mirror image of me doesn't respond. My cock jumps from my rough touch, and I slide my briefs off, taking a step back to really look at myself in the mirror.

I swallow at the sight of my erect cock, bouncing freely.

My dark hair is mussed from a night out on the town, my eyes glassy and dark.

I stand straighter as I stroke my cock, watching the way my hand glides over my shaft.

And I wonder if anyone will ever see me like this.

Naked with my cock in my hands.

My mind wanders to Saint & Sinner, to the pretty boy angel and his smooth, oiled skin. His smirk.

Telling me my songs were on his *fuck me* playlist.

I mean, who has a fuck me playlist?

People who fuck, Geo. That's who.

My own lyrics fill my brain as I let my mind wander, as I watch myself.

It's not like I'm at risk of anyone finding me or anything.

I'm a sinner, baby, and you've got me hellbent
I love the way you touch me, love the way you tease
Baby, you must be Heaven Sent

My mind is hazy as I let myself think of Rex and his warm, oiled skin, wondering what it would feel like against my own.

I bite my lip, picking up the pace. Bracing one hand against the countertop, I shift my weight, thrusting my hips.

My cock glides through my fist easily, my fingers spreading my precum over my tight cockhead.

"Oh, fuck," I curse, closing my eyes as I still.

I know this isn't what I *should* be thinking about.

Not like I jack off a lot, but when I do, I don't really think.

It's more about clearing my mind and just taking care of business.

But this... this feels different. This feels good.

I swallow, following temptation.

Fantasy is just fantasy, right?

It doesn't mean anything.

At least, that's what I tell myself.

I open my eyes, catching sight of myself, and I watch the way my hips move, slow and deliberate, as I pump my cock.

I swallow hard, but I don't stop.

I can't stop.

From this angle, it looks like I *could* be fucking someone.

"You like that?" I ask my reflection. He doesn't answer, but he doesn't have to.

I close my eyes as I imagine sliding my cock into a wet, warm mouth.

My mind wanders to Hell.

Mateo said it was gorgeous downstairs, and I wonder what Rex would look like in the tight red shorts and black harnesses the devil attendants were wearing.

I look down at him in my psyche, at the way he kneels before me. Waiting.

I'm so close.

So fucking close.

My pace quickens, but it isn't enough.

I groan, because this is how it always is.

Getting there isn't easy, even when I want to. And I want to.

So fucking bad.

I miss you.

The voice that fills my head is familiar. Soft, but masculine.

Different than the voice I remember, but somehow similar still.

Sparkling green eyes gaze up at me, and Rex disappears.

Bright green eyes framed by black eyeliner and thick lashes. Eyes I knew very well, once.

I bite my lip, squeezing my eyes shut.

But it's no use.

My alcohol-ridden brain chases the rabbit as my cock throbs and my rhythm starts to become a bit erratic.

"Show me how bad you missed me," I grit between my teeth, chasing my elusive orgasm.

I come. Hard, and fast.

"Fuck!" I curse as the guilt settles. I open my eyes, my breath coming in rapid pants, my heart filling with panic and anxiety. I catch my flushed face in the mirror as I hold my hand over my pulsing cock.

God, forgive me.

I try to stifle the guilt, the shame.

This is the part I hate.

The aftermath.

There's no one here to hold me, to make it better. There is only the deafening silence, and the harsh truth I don't want to face.

That I am defective.

I let the water wash me of my sins, burying them in the darkest parts of myself.

CHAPTER 5

GEO

MY ALARM GOES off like a screeching siren, rousing me from the depths of hell.

I groan, shoving my face into my pillow. My head is splitting, my mouth is dry, and I need to piss like a damn racehorse.

I let out an aggravated sigh, knowing that no matter how badly I want to hibernate in my warm bed, the alarm isn't going to shut itself off.

Rolling over, I grab my phone, silencing the ringer. I grab my glasses off the nightstand, putting them on and checking my messages.

I see a couple missed calls. One from Hailee, one from Jinger, three from Kevin, and…

My body tenses when I see the call *I made.*

Zeb.

I suck in a breath, realizing I fucked up.

Oh no.

Oh no no no…

I rack my brain, trying to remember last night, but I only wince at the pain beckoning in my skull.

That's what you get for downing a whole bottle of champagne, idiot.

I groan in agony. My dick doesn't seem to care that I drunk-dialed my former bandmate and ex-best friend last night, and as such, I swing my legs over the side of the bed and get my ass moving to the damn bathroom.

"What the fuck were you thinking?" I mumble as I make my way into the bathroom.

I brace one arm out against the wall and hang my head in shame.

Ten years.

It's been ten years since I have spoken to Zeb, not that I haven't thought about calling him.

After I left for Hollywood, I wanted to call him.

A lot.

Every talk show booked, every live performance, every sold out show, I wanted to call him.

I wanted to share my success with *him*.

But Zeb and I viewed "success" very differently.

I didn't want to make music without him, but he was just nineteen, and hadn't really performed on his own, and he didn't want to sell out. He didn't understand that it wasn't selling out. Not to me. I'd worked my whole life for that record deal, and I wasn't going to let anything get in the way of what I wanted more than anything.

So, I told him fine. I told him I didn't need him.

I didn't need anyone. I'd make it on my own.

And I thought about that day, thought about him often, because it's the one thing I regret about choosing this life.

That I fucked over the one person who mattered more than anyone else in the grand scheme of things. My best friend, my music partner.

I finish up with my hour long piss, washing my hands anxiously.

What the fuck did I say to him?

I don't even remember.

One look back at my phone shows me that our conversation lasted thirty-five minutes.

What the fuck were we talking about for thirty-five minutes at two in the morning?

I run a hand through my hair, biting my lip as Kevin texts me.

Saw your photos from last night. Gotta say, Geo, hitting up Saint & Sinner was genius.

I bite my fingernail, worried about what he might have seen. What I might have done.

Memories flash hazily in my mind of angel boys in tight shorts, one specifically, who I'm ninety-nine percent sure was hitting on me.

Which is weird, because I'm not gay.

I mean, I'm famously straight.

And a fucking virgin.

Maybe he thought I was someone else.

I know as I try to convince myself, it's just desperation. I sigh as Kevin sends another text through.

Sure enough, there's me, Mateo, and Dare all hanging out in the booth with our glasses of champagne.

Well, and Dare and his overflowing glass of strawberries, too.

Thankfully, the photos don't show anything except me drinking, which is a huge relief. No angel boys in tight pants to be seen.

Thank the lord.

I'm sure whatever had my briefs in a twist was probably just the amount of alcohol in my system.

Right?

I stare at the number in my call log, those three little letters heavy and magnetic.

Zeb.

I debate if I should call him. On the one hand, I could just... not. Pretend it never happened; move on with my life because it was a mistake. Unintentional.

People drunk dial their exes and stuff all the time.

Right?

I mean, he's not my *ex* in the typical sense. Ex-best friend, maybe. But not like... an ex ex, like Tiffany.

God, I should just call him, right?

That way I'll know. If I said something stupid, at least I can apologize, and if I didn't, well, maybe at least he can fill in the blanks.

Hopefully, I didn't spill anything he can leak

to the press. Not that I think Zeb would ever do something like that, but I did kind of fuck him over, so who knows.

My finger hovers over the number and I consider pressing it.

Ten years.

Thirty-five minutes.

It's just a fucking phone call, for God's sake!

I hit the button, immediately panicking. Anxiety swells in my chest as it rings, and I think maybe I should just hang up and...

"Hey." Zeb's voice brings everything back.

Fucking everything.

My cheeks flush, my blood heats, and my cock stiffens and I have to resist the urge to curse.

"Hey," I reply, gripping the phone a little tighter.

"Rough night?" Zeb asks, and I can hear the humor in his voice.

His voice is deeper, smoother. Like hot fudge.

He also sounds less... sleepy.

"Something like that," I say, noting the time on my alarm clock. It's eleven thirty. Fuck! I'm usually in the studio by ten! I need to get the fuck moving.

"Fuck!" I curse, immediately realizing my error. "Sorry, I didn't mean to—I just... my head is fucking killing me, and I'm like an hour and a half late for the studio."

"Mhmm," he murmurs, the sarcasm evident in his tone. "Did you at least have fun?"

I sigh, hopping into a fresh pair of blue jeans. I let out a nervous laugh. "Um, I don't remember."

It's not a lie.

I don't remember much, except...

My gaze travels to the bathroom, the mirror staring back at me like a suspicious Bond villain.

I force the thoughts of my fantasies away. No, I will not go down that road. It was a one time thing.

Because of the alcohol. Because clearly, I was fucked up and my brain wasn't working right.

Right?

"Listen, uh, whatever I said last night, I—"

"I know," Zeb says, his tone shifting from humorous and sarcastic to bitter.

"Know what?" I ask, feeling on the spot. I put him on speaker as I reach for a clean shirt and pull it on.

"You didn't mean to call me," he grunts.

I don't miss the venom behind his voice, and I think whatever it was I said must have been pretty bad. Regret floods me.

"Yeah. I was just, uh—"

"Drunk. Yeah, I know. It happens." I can hear him moving around. A door opens and shuts, the whir of what sounds like a coffee pot is ambient noise.

He sighs, his tone shifting just the slightest. "I'm sorry, too."

I pull on my watch, glancing at the phone, at his name.

A part of me feels like he's here, but he's not.

And he'll *never* be here. Here isn't where he belongs; he made that more than clear ten years ago.

"For what?" I ask, my heart in my throat.

Am I such a glutton for punishment?

"For what it's worth, it *sounded* like you had fun." His tone is softer, but it's still smooth and comforting.

Still masculine and strong.

It's not all that different when he sings.

Or when he used to sing, when it was just the two of us.

I was always trying to get him to perform

more. Technically, he was hired to be my guitarist for my band, but after a night cosmic bowling with some friends at the time, I knew more people needed to hear him *sing.*

His voice is amazing. It's like Sleep Token, but sexier.

If that's even possible.

"I really am sorry. I mean, it was like two-thirty in the morning."

Zeb lets out a dark chuckle. "Look at you staying out past your bedtime," he teases me.

My heart thuds like a drum in my chest.

I miss this.

I miss him.

Us.

I miss my best friend.

"Yeah, well, don't get excited. I don't plan on a repeat anytime soon." I slide my boots on, run my hands through my hair with a quick spritz of product, and take a look at myself in the mirror.

One look and I immediately make for my makeup bag and dig for my concealer. My eyes look fucking wrecked.

"Drink some coffee, take some ibuprofen, and eat some bacon, you'll be just fine."

"Seriously, who in their right mind does this

shit more than once?" I reach for my contacts, omitting my thick tortoise-shell glasses. I pat the concealer under my eyes. I learned early on that if I just viewed all of this as a costume, or a uniform, it was easier.

Being *Gravedigger* is a job like anything else. It's not that different from the image I used to have to portray when I was just Geo Graves.

It just feels different because I'm famous now and I go by *Gravedigger* instead, and traded in my polos and khakis for abs, ripped jeans, and leather jackets.

I cock my head to the side, taking in my appearance once more.

Better.

"Really? You the leading consultant on hang-overs now, Z?" I put my makeup and products back in their bag and give one last tousle of my dark hair.

I don't miss the way his name rolls off my tongue. Familiar.

Even though I haven't said it out loud in years.

"I might know a thing or two," he says, his voice apathetic.

"Right. I, uh... got to head out to studio, but, uh..."

I swallow, my heart again in my throat because I know I should hang up, but I don't want to.

"Can I call you? Later, I mean? Catch up, maybe?"

For a moment, I think we have disconnected because there is nothing but silence.

Then I hear him let out a long, deep breath.

"Yeah. I guess," he says, but his voice seems different. Guarded.

"Cool," I say, nodding as I bound down the steps, toward my garage.

"Cool," he says.

I grab my keys to my Lexus, and the sound of the locks whirring echoes in the room.

He doesn't hang up. I take a deep breath and hit end call, if only because I do need to head out, and I know if I don't...

Fuck, I might just forget that I'm a complete and total asshole where Zeb Ingram is concerned. Shit, I might forget that we're not even friends anymore.

And what's more dangerous than that?

CHAPTER 6

Zeb

I should not have answered the damn phone. I should have let it go to voicemail, or ignored it, but I'd be lying if I said I wasn't waiting for that call.

Because I knew he'd call.

To apologize, tidy things back up. That's how Geo operates.

Though, I guess I can't blame him because I'd probably be the same way if I grew up the way he did.

The Graves aren't bad people by any means,

but Geo never really got the chance to just be a teenager like his sister.

His mom started signing him up for gigs on the Christian Rock circuit when he was just thirteen, and soon enough, Geo Graves was on his way to stardom.

I remember seeing him for the first time when I went over their house to hang out with his sister, Katy. We were fifteen.

Fucking hell, he was so pretty.

Tall, kinda nerdy, if I'm being honest. He looked like some amalgamation of a Disney prince and boy bander. By twenty-five he was the perfect dream.

Katy was the one they let get away with murder, because she was the girl. And the baby, of course.

Geo was held to higher standards because he was a boy, and he was the oldest.

"You need to set a good example," his mother would say, as if he *were* a child, when he was a fucking adult.

But he took his role seriously. For his sister, his family, his fans.

Even though it meant he had to put himself, his wants, his needs last.

Which is why even as pissed as I was that he left all those years ago for Hollywood, I understood why he did it.

He wanted the lights for himself. He wanted to be more than Geo Graves.

He wanted to be *Gravedigger*.

He wanted to break *free*.

I just wanted him, and I didn't have the fucking balls to tell him the truth.

And somehow, here I am, ten years later, and it's like nothing's changed.

Except, everything has changed.

I know I should have told him no, when he asked to call me later.

But I'm weak, when it comes to Geo Graves.

I mean, he *says* he'll call, but he'll probably forget. I shouldn't get my hopes up.

What I *should* do, is get my shit together, because as I look at my watch, I note I have about ten minutes if I want to leave and pick Katy up on time for my gig at the *Flower Festival* today.

Katy's always been my ride or die, since the eighth grade. She was the reason I got the gig playing with Geo in the first place, and she was the one in my corner pushing me to keep making music on my own after he left.

She was also the first person I came out to, officially, after I turned twenty-one.

Sure enough, just as I manage to grab my phone, wallet, and keys, and head for the truck, she texts me.

Can we stop and get Starbies on the way, Z? Dad drank the last of my Sumatra Reserve.

I roll my eyes, shaking my head.

Damn the Graves.

Damn them all.

Depends. You buying me a coffee, too? I text her a pleading eyes emoji, and when she texts me back an emoji eye roll with the word, *fine*, I feel a little better.

Hey, I'm a starving musician, remember?

I slide into my truck, turning the radio on, the sound blaring loudly.

I freeze for a moment as familiar vocals fill my space, and I know I should change the channel.

Cast out on the edges
Looking for a sign
Heaven didn't want me, baby
Because I wanted you to be mine

His voice is dark and raspy, with that breathy

edge that just oozes sex appeal. But it's changed, too, over the years. It's not as crisp or clean sounding as it used to be before he became *Gravedigger*.

There's pain, and guilt etched in his voice, now. His pitch rises as he croons on about needing an angel, about needing to find salvation.

I turn the radio dial, because I just can't stand to listen to his perfect voice filling my speakers right now. I need to get Geo Graves out of my head, and focus on my music.

Because I know at least that's the one thing that will never hurt me.

I PULL UP TO THE GRAVES' residence, and I text Katy.

Joel, their dad, comes barreling around the side of the house dragging a giant cooler toward the trailer parked in the driveway, and I don't think twice about shutting the car off, and jumping out to help.

"Let me help you with that, Mr. Graves," I say, nudging him out the way. Sometimes it pays to be the bigger guy who can throw his weight around.

"Thanks, Zeb," he says, sucking in a deep breath. "You know how Debbie gets when the trailer isn't stocked." He rolls his eyes.

I do know.

At one point, she stocked the trailer with my favorite snacks, too.

I hoist the cooler up, following him to the trailer as he opens the door.

"You know you could have just ridden with us," he says cautiously.

I sigh, because this isn't the first time we've had this conversation, and I know it's not going to be the last.

"I appreciate the offer, Mr. Graves, really I do, but—" I drop the cooler, just as I hear Katy bounding out of the door.

"What are you doing in *there*?" she says as she hangs in the doorway.

Her auburn hair is pulled up into a messy bun, adorned with flowers and feathers, and she looks every bit like she's heading to Coachella instead of the Tucson Flower Festival.

Mr. Graves glances between the two of us, before sighing.

I know at one point when we were teenagers, her parents thought we were going to end up married with a white picket fence, three point five kids, and a dog, because we were *always* together. Practically joined at the hip, most of the time.

But even then, I knew I wasn't interested in girls, and Katy knew, too. Even if I didn't say anything. Sometimes, I think she knew I was gay before I did, if I'm being honest.

"Being a gentleman, of course," I tease her.

She rolls her eyes. "A gentleman would buy *me* a coffee." She sticks her tongue out at me.

"I told you. Starving musician," I rile her.

Mr. Graves chuckles, and I hear his wife chattering on the phone. I know we all need to get the hell out of dodge if we want to make it to this festival on time.

I hop down from the step as Katy steps back. In the sun, the glitter on her cheeks sparkles.

"Come on." I nod toward my truck.

As soon as I turn the radio on, I hear Geo singing. Again.

That same song I heard on my way over her, *Heaven Sent.*

How many times in an hour are they playing this thing?

I move to change the channel, but Katy stops me.

"Leave it," she says, and I don't have the heart to argue with her.

"Fine."

I lean one arm on my windowsill while I palm the steer wheeling, focusing on the drive ahead as Katy texts on her phone.

"What's up?" I ask, raising an eyebrow because I can see she's pretty focused, and usually, she's talking my ear off the minute I pick her up.

Technically, I don't need a manager anymore. I'm a one man act, and as such, I like to be in control of where I play, what I play, and what I write.

After Geo left, that was it. His mother was pissed; hell, we all were.

But I was just the guitarist then, and I didn't want to perform anything without him. Eventually, his mother picked up other acts over the years.

Katy was the only one who listened to all my stupid, heartbroken songs then. She was the only one I played for, and finally, after years of playing for her, one day at college, she told me she'd booked me a gig.

Now, she's more like my assistant than a manager. She runs my booth, posts on social media, and sometimes, she even buys me coffee.

Honestly, I don't know what I'd do without her, sometimes.

"Mom said Cora Cozette canceled last minute because she lost her voice," she says, looking up at me with a grin.

I raise my eyebrow. "And that's good?" I ask, a little dumbfounded because usually, when someone is sick, that isn't smile-worthy.

"Um... yeah, Zeb. She was headlining, so..."

I pull through the Starbucks drive-thru, rattling off Katy's usual grande oatmilk mocha and my usual nitro cold brew. When I pull through to the window, she smugly responds, "Mom said she talked to the event coordinator and now *you're* headlining."

My blood heats at her words.

Headlining? Me?

I can't hide my shock. Partly because, well, it's a reach even for her.

Debbie Graves barely acknowledges that I

have a music career, despite the fact we see her and her new protégés all the time on the circuit.

"Is this a trick?" I glance at her, knowing the doubt is written on my face.

Katy shakes her head as the attendant hands us our drinks through the window and I give her my payment card.

Katy smirks at me. "Thought you were a starving artist," she touts, taking a sip of her drink.

The woman hands me back my card and I thank her.

"That was earlier. Now I'm a headliner," I say with a grin. "Besides, I told you, I'm a gentleman."

Katy laughs, and I can't help but laugh, too.

"More like a gentle giant, but I'll take it," she says, and I can't help but laugh, too.

"We should put some glitter on you, too, *headliner*," she teases.

I nod. "Sure. Go for it."

It wouldn't be the first time, that's for sure. Katy's been dolling me up for years for events.

I don't miss the excitement in her voice. "Yes! You're going to dazzle them all, darling."

Maybe today won't be so bad after all.

THE CROWD at the festival was a lot bigger than I anticipated, but I'm sure it's nothing compared to what Geo is used to.

Still, it takes a good bit of energy and focus to keep the energy moving, but thankfully, the request part of my set always does a good job bridging the gap and ending the set.

Usually, folks will request the karaoke staples, like *Don't Stop Believing, Sweet Caroline,* or even *Don't Go Breaking My Heart.* Sometimes, though, at events like this, they'll request popular songs, especially lately, because Katy's been loading acoustic videos of me covering popular songs onto my YouTube.

But nothing could have prepared me for the request to play *Heaven Sent.*

I look at Katy, who just gives me a thumbs up.

Big help she is.

I could just tell them I don't know the song, but I also don't want to end this set on a note that leaves people dissatisfied, either.

So, I suck up my pride, my guilt, and the

anxiety swimming in my stomach at the thought of Geo, and I do it.

I play *his* song.

I know all the lyrics, because I've heard it a hundred times over, even when I try to avoid it.

Like I've tried to avoid everything *Gravedigger* puts out, because it hurts.

It reminds me of what I *lost*.

"You're the devil, baby, and I just want to be blessed," I sing.

My heart aches with every line, because out of all his songs, this one just hits different.

Because it feels personal, even though I know it isn't.

"I want to drown in you, baby, because you're *Heaven Sent*."

I steal a glance at Katy, watching as her eyes widen and she holds her hand over her heart.

"So good," she mouths to me.

The crowd cheers and I bow, taking my leave.

"You sounded amazing out there, Zeb," she says.

I force a smile. Because all I want to do is forget how those words make me feel.

CHAPTER 7

ZEB

AFTER DROPPING Katy off to meet some friends for dinner, I bow out.

Not that I have anything against Katy's friends or anything, I mean I consider some of them my friends, too, but I just want to go home, order some Door Dash, and curl up on my couch for a bit.

I know it's probably stupid to get all bent out of shape over a *song*.

But it's not just a song, to me. It's the embodiment of everything that never was and never will be.

I'd written something similar, eleven years ago.

It was called *Hellbound*.

I wrote songs like crazy during those three years we worked together, and Geo was always interested in what I was writing. Every time I saw him, he asked if I was working on something, or begged me to play for him, and every time, it was like a hundred balloon salute.

He had no idea my songs were about him, and that every time I serenaded him, I was putting my stupid heart out there.

And every time he'd grin, his eyes shining with pride and excitement like I was *it*. Like I was a star.

And I held on to every smile, every word of praise like it was fucking air.

But his favorite was *Hellbound*.

I get lost in the memories for a few minutes. Mourning what could've been if only I'd had the balls.

"It would be fun to do a double album. Hellbound and Heaven Sent," he said.

"The artwork would be sick! Can you imagine? Just like one could be all black with glowing

neon devil horns," I replied as I grabbed my sketchbook. "Oh! Maybe a swishy devil tail."

"Oh! The Heaven Sent one could have neon blue angel wings. And a halo," he gushed, his eyes shining.

"Heaven Sent could have all these religious undertones, too. You know, go all in on the heavenly metaphors."

Geo strummed away on his guitar, his glasses sliding down his nose just a fraction and the corners of his lips perked up in a smile. He always looked sexy as hell when he smiled like that.

"You'd have to write all the Hellbound songs, though," he demanded as I sketched away some angel and devil wings next to him.

He leaned back, the motion making the couch cushions dip just a fraction, which put us closer together.

I nonchalantly leaned back against the cushions behind us, and he didn't move.

I could smell his sweet orange blossom and spice scent. I glanced up for the fraction of a moment, noting the slender expanse of his exposed neck, the curve of his Adam's Apple. I stopped sketching.

"*Why do you say that?*" I asked, swallowing hard.

I watched his long fingers play with the strings, his touch delicate and precise. His hands, the perfect design. Calloused from playing, but supremely hot when you watch him do it. The way his fingers glide, the way the muscles and joints move, making the veins stand out.

I thought about those hands often, wondering what they'd feel like in my hair. Around my neck.

"*Because you're the expert, of course,*" he says lightly.

I let out a nervous laugh.

"*You calling me a demon, Geo?*"

Geo turned toward me, the motion making his thigh brush against mine. He smirked. "If the shoe fits, Z." His dark, amber gaze implored me as he handed me his guitar.

I took it from his hands, as he glanced at it.

"*Play for me,*" *he ordered.*

I bit my lip, because I knew I should say no. I sank a little closer to him as he leaned his arm against the back cushion, shifting once more, turning toward me.

"*Please?*"

He watched me with interest, and I knew I couldn't say no.

How could I when he looked at me like that?

"What do you want to hear?" I asked.

"Hellbound," he said, leaning his head against his palm. His amber eyes sparkled as he smiled softly. "It's my favorite."

I smiled and nodded as I strummed out the chords.

"Heaven won't take me because I'm a sinner

Earth won't keep me on the ground

My heart wants to fly beyond its cage

I want to scream but I can't make a sound

Because every time you look at me, baby, I know I'm Hellbound."

I pull up to my house, the sun lighting up the sky in shades of ochre and violet, casting a golden glow on my memories.

I set about to making myself something to eat instead of ordering out, if only because cooking usually helps keep me busy enough my thoughts won't wander.

I glance at the clock as I chop some avocado for my burrito bowl, noting it's nearing seven.

He hasn't called.

And I doubt he's going to.

Once I'm finished with my chopping, I turn on my Spotify and play some fast-paced emo music. I get undressed, grab a beer, and relax on my couch with my laptop, my phone on the cushion next to me.

I scroll through social media absentmindedly, stopping when I come across an article shared in Vanity Fair from last month featuring the musicians from the *Pillars Of Rock* tour.

Geo looks up at me from the photo in the post, alongside his label mates—*Felix Heart*, *Mage Of Mercy*, and *Heart Killer*.

I stop, my fingers hovering over the group photo. He looks so different now than the man I remember.

Gone are the cute thick glasses and the messy blond-brown hair, that boyish smile.

But his eyes are the same.

Deep, rich amber eyes that pull me in like a magnet.

I click through the photos, until I get to his solo set, because I truly am a glutton for punishment.

I swallow as my fingers touch the screen.

He stands before me, those perfect hands on his hips. Decked out in bracelets, and a familiar shiny, silver ring, somehow, they look hotter. If that's possible.

My gaze travels across his torso, noting the definition of his hips. His fucking *six pack* beneath his ink.

A giant black cross that covers his chest and torso.

My gaze travels down to his tapered waist, to his tight black, ripped jeans and bare feet.

I stopped looking up Geo nine years ago, because I didn't want to be reminded of what was one of the worst days of my life, and my first real heartbreak.

I didn't want to see him, because it hurt to look at him.

But now...

Now, I can't take my eyes off of him.

My cock twitches in my boxers, and I suck in a heavy breath.

I always thought Geo was attractive, but now...

It's like he truly went from *Heaven Sent* to *Hellbound*.

I slip my hand beneath my waistband, if only to adjust my cock, and I notice a bead of wetness pebbling my cockhead.

I swallow harshly, swiping my thumb across the tip, if only to remove it, but the touch only makes it worse.

My gaze fixates on Geo's photograph, the way he's cocked his head, showcasing his not-so-slender-anymore neck. His shoulders are thicker, his frame fuller, defined.

He gazes at me through his dark lashes, amber eyes rimmed in kohl liner.

Those perfect, pouty lips parted just enough.

My cock throbs and my hips move of their own accord, eliciting a guilty groan from my throat.

I shouldn't fucking do this.

It's wrong on so many levels, and I know it's not good for me.

But it's not like anyone is going to suddenly walk in on me and find me like this.

I'm a single man who lives alone.

Maybe just this once. For old time's sake.

My gaze dips to the tagline below the image which boasts, "Get Undressed With *Gravedigger*: Sex, Love, & Rock 'N' Roll."

Without thinking, I click on the hyperlink, which brings me to a page with a much larger image of Geo.

Lying down on a velvet couch, his arm behind his head, showcasing thick biceps with prominent veins, his dark eyes staring at me, those perfect full lips.

Fuck, that's hot.

I lean back, pulling my cock out as I press my lips together.

I close my eyes, trying to focus on building a slow, steady rhythm, but I can't focus.

I open my eyes, staring at his image. At the way his tattoo spans across his defined pecs, how the bottom of the cross doesn't stop at the waistband of his jeans. It goes *below* the waistband, and I find myself wondering where it ends.

I never would have dreamed in a million years Geo would be the guy with a giant tattoo that covers his entire chest and torso, but I can't deny that it's sexy as hell.

The thought of tracing those lines with my tongue—across his pecs, down his abs, below his fucking waistband—pushes through my psyche and I let out another grunt of guilt.

I think about those perfect hands, fingers threaded through my hair, pushing me down on his cock.

I knew Geo was a virgin when we met. I

never judged him for it, even though he was older, because it made sense. His family was pretty religious, and he was a popular Christian artist.

But I'd be lying if I said I didn't fantasize about driving my mouth over his fucking cock and showing him what Heaven really felt like, even if he was way out of my league.

I close my eyes once more as the familiar fantasy resurfaces and my breath catches in my throat as I let myself succumb to it.

I imagine my fingers gripping his thighs, my tongue swiping across his slit, tasting the salty sweetness of his precum.

I let myself imagine those calloused fingers gripping my hair as he thrusts himself into the back of my throat.

My thrusts come faster, harder, and the sound of wet skin slapping against my palm echoes in the empty, quiet space of my living room

"Oh, fuck," I curse as my muscles tighten, my abs spasming as I erupt like a volcano.

A deep moan escapes me as warm, thick cum sprays onto my abdomen, and I curse.

Just as the phone rings.

Panic sets in, and I move for my phone, ready to silence it, because I can't do this right now, I can't...

But my hands are slippery and the damn thing falls right off my couch, onto the floor, and...

"Hello?" Geo's voice echoes in the space as I bury my face in my pillow, my cock still pulsing, still squirting out the remains of my guilty release.

I let out a petulant groan.

If God exists, why does he hate me so fucking much?

"Zeb, are you there?" he asks, his voice like warm sugar.

"Yeah. Yeah, I'm here," I say as I lift my head, looking at the ceiling.

I should have just hung up when I had the chance.

CHAPTER 8

Geo

For a moment, I wonder if this was a bad idea.

But it's just a phone call, right?

Plenty of people call each other, have normal conversations.

So why does this feel so... not like that?

Maybe it has to do with the fact that the entire day at the studio, I couldn't *think* straight.

Kevin had written up a *list* of clubs like Saint & Sinner that he felt would "help my image", but I told him it didn't matter. I wasn't going to be going out to another sex club any time soon.

Because if anything, the experience made me realize how fucking out place I am not just there, but...

What the fuck am I doing?

With this tour?

With Casualty?

With my life?

Then again, I guess every thirty-nine year old on the cusp of the big four-oh gets gifted an existential crisis, right?

Even playing my songs just doesn't feel the same, but I hit my marks. I always do, because at least I know if there is *one* thing I can do, it's music.

I've always felt the most at home, the most confident on stage, with a microphone. There's a realness to performing for me, that doesn't exist anywhere in my life.

No matter what costume I'm donning—Geo Graves, boy next door or *Gravedigger*, rockstar— when I step on the stage, when I grab that microphone I'm me.

There's only one other place I've ever felt that at home, that authentic, and I know I'll never have *that* again.

"You, uh, is this a bad time?" I ask, Zeb's

heavy breaths in my ear making me feel a bit flushed.

I adjust my cock, because clearly it's got a mind of its own these days.

Maybe it's having a pre-forty existential crisis, too.

"No, it's fine," he says, letting out a sigh. The tinge of gravel in his voice has returned, and I swallow hard.

God, why am I so hot all of a sudden?

"It's, uh… good to hear your voice," I say, like an idiot.

I mean, it is true. It is nice to hear him, but clearly not talking for ten years has only made me forget how to actually hold a conversation.

It's just Zeb. Conversation should be easy. It was always easy before.

I can hear movement on the other end of the phone as I undress myself, crawling into bed.

I know being in bed before nine o'clock is like a kiss of death for most people, and as a rockstar, I'm supposed to be out at places like Saint & Sinner having the fucking time of my life.

But something about this—curling up my covers, listening to Zeb's voice—this feels a thousand times better than being drunk at Saint & Sinner.

Zeb lets out another long sigh, his voice softer. "Yeah. It's good to hear your voice too, G."

A smile threatens to form on my lips as I get comfortable.

"How..." He pauses, and for a moment I feel panicked.

"How did it go at the... studio today?" he asks, his tone shifting, his deep, smooth voice full of caution.

A part of me knows I should be careful, because this—calling him, pretending we're *friends* again, falling back into his orbit—is too tempting.

On speaker, his voice fills the room, and it feels like he's here.

And if I close my eyes, I can pretend he is.

So, I close my eyes, my shoulders relaxing as I lean back in bed, and I answer him.

"It sucked, actually," I say with a sigh. Something about that confession, as mundane and dull as it is, feels like I've shattered glass.

Like I've broken a barrier of some sort.

Zeb shifts, and I hear his deep breath again as he asks. "Do you want to talk about it?"

His words are careful, but I don't miss the familiarity in them, either.

My mind wanders for a moment to all those days Zeb showed up for practice, clearly pissed off or bothered by something that happened at school.

My mother always said in order to get anywhere in any career, you needed to leave your shit at the door.

When I walked through the door of the studio, or the trailer, or set foot on a stage, there was no room to be distracted or bogged down by angst and drama, as she said.

But I always thought if I could have talked about what was on my mind *before* I assumed my role as Geo Graves, maybe it would have helped me sort my shit out better.

So, any time Zeb came rolling through those doors with tight shoulders or a glazed look in his eye, I made him tell me what was wrong so we could move past it and focus on our music together. I wanted to give him the space he needed because he was my bandmate, but also because, well, I wanted to make him feel better, if I could.

Pissed off, angry or frustrated Zeb always made me feel the worst. Like even though I knew it wasn't possible, it felt like it was my fault somehow, and I wanted to make it better.

I know I shouldn't go down the road of Hollywood gripes with the man I left for Hollywood, but something about the familiarity of his voice, mixed with that soothing, almost hypnotic deep breath... I just can't help myself.

"It's just this tour, I guess. We kick off in a few weeks, and I'm just... I think I'm having a mid-life crisis or something."

He chuckles, the sound smooth and warm. It makes me feel a fraction better.

"You know, technically, you don't *know* if you're middle aged. Because no one knows when they're going to die. You could die in like ten years, and middle aged at that point would have been twenty-five."

I roll my eyes as I lay down in bed, getting comfortable on my side, propping my elbow up so I can rest my head in my palm.

"So what you're saying is I'm already ancient. Thanks, Z."

Zeb chuckles. "No, I'm just saying the whole being middle-aged thing is subjective."

"Pretty sure forty is middle-aged, Zeb, but thanks."

His voice lifts a fraction, and I can hear the humor in it. "You're not forty yet, G. Still got a month."

I blink as I let his words settle on me.

"A month until I'm the literal forty-year-old virgin," I gripe. "Yeah, can't wait."

There's a moment of silence before his soft, smooth voice comes across the line.

"Could be worse," he says.

I let out a sarcastic laugh. "Oh yeah, how could it be worse?"

"Well, you could be a perverted, creepy old man with a shriveled up dick."

"I'm definitely not a perverted, creepy old man," I huff. "And my dick is certainly not *shriveled*, thank you very much."

Zeb laughs, and the sound is like melted better. Deep, warm, and dare I say... sexy?

"No, you are definitely not pervy, creepy, or old." His voice is light, but there is an edge to it. He coughs slightly, his voice rich with humor.

"What about you?" I ask as I settle down lower, laying my head on the pillow.

"What about me?" he asks.

"How was... your day?" I ask, getting comfortable.

I absentmindedly adjust my cock again. I swear this thing has a mind of its own. Now is *not* the time, buddy!

There's a pause before he answers. "It was okay, for the most part. I guess."

"No existential crisis because your thirtieth is around the corner?"

"No," he says softly. "Just another day in boring old Posdosh."

I don't miss the sadness or the guilt in his voice.

"Besides, thirty isn't the death of my youth or anything."

I can't resist the urge to tease him just a bit.

"So you're not some middle-aged, pervy, creepy old man with a shriveled dick, either?" I snap, my lips turning up into a smile.

"Fuck, no," he says with a resounding rebuttal. "Thirty is the new twenty, haven't you heard?" he taunts.

I scoff at his remark, but I can't help smiling.

I can't remember the last time I felt this good just *talking* to someone.

It's not just someone, it's Zeb.

"Can't say that I have," I say, and we both catch our breaths. There is a pregnant pause, a tense silence.

"Can I ask you something?" I say, swallowing harshly. Panic floods me, but I know I need to say this, because I've been thinking about it all day, and I don't want to let him slip through my fingers again.

I was always raised to believe God lets things happen for a reason, and I think maybe that reason is he's giving me a chance to make amends.

"Sure," Zeb says, his voice a bit more relaxed.

I glance at the clock, noting it's nearing ten thirty.

"*Pillars* is scheduled to make a stop in Tucson, and I'll have a couple days before and after the show before we have to bound off to Georgia," I start.

Suddenly, I feel nervous he's going to say no.

And this... this conversation is going to end, and I don't want it to.

"Oh," he says quietly.

"I was thinking, maybe... and I'd totally understand if, like... you didn't want to, but, I was *hoping*—"

His voice drops an octave, and my cock twitches. *Again.*

"Hoping for what, Geo?"

I don't realize that I've stopped talking altogether, because all I can focus on is the sound of his hot fudge sundae voice.

"I was hoping, uh... maybe we could... catch up? Have lunch or something?"

"You want to catch up? With me?" I don't miss the way his voice lifts, like he's nervous. Though, I guess I can't blame him.

"Yes," I say quietly.

There is a pause, and for a moment, I think he's hung up. But then he speaks.

"Okay." His voice is soft, and he sounds sleepy.

I yawn in response. "Okay," I murmur as I bury my face in my pillow.

"Go to sleep, Geo." His voice is deep, smooth, suggestive, and with that added gravel of sleepiness, I can't help but let out a contented sigh.

I've never felt so warm.

He said okay. Maybe I can fix things after all.

"Okay," I answer, but I don't hang up.

"Okay," he breathes.

I focus on the sound of his breath, the rhythm of it, and before I know it, I'm out like a light.

MY PHONE SCREECHES at the tender hour of six am, and I groan into my pillow, realizing my glasses are still on my fucking face.

I sit up, adjusting them. Thankfully, they aren't too bent.

I reach for the phone to shut it off, seeing a couple texts and a call from my sister.

Call me back, asshole!

Seriously, you can't avoid me forever!

Don't make me call Kevin!

She's right, I can't keep avoiding her, but I'm not ready to have the *home* conversation.

I haven't been home since I left. My leaving left a lot of people upset, including my parents.

My mom had been my manager for sixteen years, and she had no clue that I'd sent in a package to Casualty Records. The only person that knew I was even *looking* at other options was Katy.

Zeb knew I wanted to be famous—mainstream famous—but we didn't really talk about my dreams of Hollywood, because he didn't seem to really favor the idea of "selling out".

But I don't think anyone was more shocked about my departure than my mom.

I love my parents, I really do, but I needed to leave the nest in more ways than one, and if I told them I *wanted to leave*, they would have just found a way to stop it from happening. So, I didn't tell them I was leaving until I was on my way to the airport. I have worked pretty hard to avoid going back to Arizona until now, but Casualty chose the cities for this tour, not me.

My gaze catches the call below my missed call from my sister. Three little letters call out to me, and I bite my lip as I debate whether or not to avoid my sister altogether and call *him* instead.

Then I notice the call log time. Twelve thirty.

I blink, knowing I was definitely asleep before eleven.

I know I didn't hang up, but... why didn't he?

Maybe he fell asleep and hung up after he woke up. Yeah, I'm sure that's what happened.

My memory slides back to our conversation last night.

His smooth, warm voice, his rhythmic, deep breaths.

I sigh, feeling the weight of my cock in my briefs as it twitches, needing attention.

Is this the beginning of my creepy, perverted old man era?

Do you just turn forty and your dick and your brain become separate entities?

Or is this because my dick is having an existential crisis of his own?

I slide my briefs down, knowing it's probably just better to take care of things now, otherwise I'll just be thinking about it for the rest of day, worried I'll pop a fucking boner at the wrong time in the wrong place.

I settle into my sheets, getting comfortable. One of the perks of being alone is that at least I can be comfortable here, because it's my home.

It took me awhile to get comfortable with masturbating in general, because I was led to believe self-pleasure was, well, wrong.

Once my mom caught me when I was four-teen, and she freaked the fuck out.

After, my dad sat me down for a "talk", and I learned pretty quickly that what felt natural to me, wasn't something I was supposed to enjoy. Sex was for marriage and procreating, end of story.

It wasn't until I moved to LA and moved in with Mateo, that I realized how fucked up it was that my parents had effectively fucked up my adolescence by shaming me instead of educating me, all because they wanted me to uphold their noble Christian values at home and in front of the public.

Ever since then, I've made it a point to do it when I feel like I need to, and I try not to feel guilty about it, which is why I usually try to not *think* about anything.

But lately, I can't seem to clear my mind the way I used to. Instead, I find my mind wandering to thoughts of deep, steady breaths that make my cock *throb*.

I don't want to think about him, not like this. It feels wrong, but...

It also feels really fucking good.

I lean my head back against my headboard, pumping my cock as my wetness spreads.

It's just fantasy, it doesn't mean anything.

It's completely normal to think sexy thoughts when you touch yourself, Geo.

One hundred percent, completely normal.

Except, usually when thoughts make their way into my confused brain, I don't think about my ex-best friend in any capacity.

But it's like ever since the other night, since I heard his voice for the first time in ten years, it's poisoned me.

I try to shift my thoughts to something else.

Ex-girlfriends, swimsuit models, even pretty angel boys.

It doesn't help, not really. I want to come so bad, but it's difficult. Every time I get close, I can't.

I whine in defeat as I give up the fight, my gaze falling on my open en-suite bathroom door. I can see the mirror from here, and I bite my lip, knowing I shouldn't think about him like this.

But the last time I did, I came easily, and it felt *really* good.

So I close my eyes and I let the fantasy fill me again.

I miss you.

That smooth, decadent voice echoes in my brain, his deep, sexy breathing accenting the memory of watching myself fuck my own hand.

My entire body locks up and the moan that escapes me is deep.

I come hard and fast, and it feels... So. Fucking. Good.

But the euphoria dies, giving way to guilt and shame once more as I watch my cock pulse, as ropes of warm, wet cum splatter across the black ink decorating my abdomen, stark in contrast.

That's twice now.

Twice that the thought of a man has made me come easier than the thought of anything or anyone else.

But not just any man.

Zeb.

Before I can even process this startling and terrifying information, my phone rings, the unmistakable ringtone making me snap my attention back to the here and now.

I quickly use my sheet to wipe myself clean before I grab the phone and punch the green button.

"Yes, Katy?" I bite, feeling a bit on edge.

"I was getting ready to call for a wellness check," she gripes.

I purse my lips, curling my knees to my chest as I drop my forehead against them.

I don't want to do this, not now. But the alternative is not looking any better, so I figure dealing with Katy and my fucking family is probably a hundred times better than dealing with the fact that I can't stop jacking off and fantasizing about a man I haven't seen in ten years.

Yeah, I'll take my family for five hundred, Alex.

CHAPTER 9

GEO

"Absolutely not," I say as I fold myself into the driver's seat of the Lexus.

"Geo, seriously. Don't you think you're being a tad bit dramatic about this whole thing?" Katy nips.

"I have a hotel, Katy," I reply firmly.

"Yeah, a hotel that is, like, an hour away from everyone."

Which is a blessing, obviously.

"Oh, so it's fine for me to travel an hour into Posdosh, but mom can't be bothered, right?" I snap.

Katy sighs. "It's not like that Geo."

I turn my car on, once again *Heaven Sent* is playing, and I change the channel.

I never intended on releasing the damn song, but Kevin found one of my old writing journals when we were moving to the new studio last year, and thought it was completely fine to read all of my songs I'd written before I signed with the label.

Songs I never shared with anyone, not even Zeb.

"These are phenomenal, Geo. How come you don't write stuff like this now?" he asked.

I only shrugged, because I was feeling super vulnerable and embarrassed that Kevin was perusing my emo Geo Graves stuff.

When I was performing as a Christian artist, my songs were always marketed as being about God, and I never really told my mom they weren't.

But most of them were love songs about that perfect person I know exists, somewhere.

The one God chose for me, but I haven't found yet.

I frown, because *Heaven Sent* always reminds of Zeb.

I wrote it as the counterpart to his song, *Hellbound*, but no one actually knows that but me.

And if I'm being honest, *Hellbound* is so much better than *Heaven Sent*.

He probably doesn't even remember about our proposed double album. It was just an idea, at the time, and sometimes, I think if I didn't get the record deal from Casualty, maybe we would have produced it together.

Maybe we could have departed from Geo Graves and formed our own act.

But I guess I'll never know what would have been, because I chose Hollywood instead. I chose *Gravedigger*.

"Then tell me what it's like, Katy, please," I snap.

She sighs. "Just think about it at least, okay? You know it's quiet here, you can relax and not have to worry about being hounded by paps, for one thing."

I chew on my bottom lip, because she's right on that account, at least, but I don't want to tell her that. I need to stand my ground.

She pauses for a moment, her voice taking on a cautious tone. "Besides. Zeb's here."

I grind my jaw a bit at her words, because I

don't know how to respond. I know he and Katy are tighter than a peanut butter and jelly sandwich, but the last thing I want to discuss with my sister is... him.

At least right now.

Panic floods me and I wonder if this is really such a good idea.

Going home.

Seeing my family.

Seeing Zeb.

What if... what if he's just, like, being polite?

What if he doesn't really want to see me, but doesn't want to hurt my feelings?

What if I go home and nothing has changed?

What if I go home and everything has changed?

Katy's voice softens. "It's where you *should* be, Geo."

"I should be at the studio right now, Katy," I fire back harshly.

She sighs. "What are you so worried about? It's mom and dad, Geo. It's your family."

I envy the ignorance my sister has. She and I didn't have the same parents growing up.

They never grounded her or shamed her for shit.

No, instead, my sister brought home her first boyfriend at sixteen, and my parents were practically thrilled because he was "a good Christian boy", but I literally caught him feeling up my sister in the pool shed the summer before they started "dating."

Good boy, my ass.

"Yeah, and my *family* doesn't have the best track record of treating me like an adult." I huff.

"Geo..." she sighs. I can hear the sadness in her voice.

I let out an exasperated sigh. "Look, I don't want to fight about this, okay?"

Her voice softens. "I know."

I pull into the studio parking lot, park my car, and turn it off. But I don't move.

There is a thick silence before she speaks again.

"You need to forgive them, Geo," she implores, and I can hear the heartache in her voice.

I stare at the studio, thinking about her words. Thinking about home.

My life wasn't terrible by any means. I know my parents were just doing what they thought was right for me because they loved me, but just because they loved me doesn't negate the fucking *trauma* they caused me.

Every value they tried to instill on me became my armor.

And even underneath the visage of *Gravedigger*, that armor is still there, even if no one can see it.

I don't know if I can forgive them, because I can't even forgive myself.

"Katy..." I sigh.

"Just... promise me you'll *think* about it, okay?" Her voice is soft, and I can hear the emotional pain in it. "I miss you. I want to see you, too, you know."

Her words are serious, and they weigh on me heavily. Suddenly, I feel like an asshole.

I might have issues with my parents, but Katy's different.

And I miss her, too. Her and Zeb, they were always my pillars of strength.

"I'll think about it, okay?" I say, swallowing harshly as my heart catches in my throat.

"Okay," she says, and then the line goes dead.

I cue up my text, and I don't even think twice about texting Zeb, even though I know I shouldn't.

But I feel overwhelmed, angry, and upset, and I need my friend. I need him.

Call you later?

I lick my lips, waiting.

I count to one, to two, until I hit ten seconds, and then I see the bubbles.

The relief that floods me is instant.

Yeah, sure.

I stare at those two words, noting how just the sight of them is a weight off my shoulders.

Maybe going home won't be so bad.

Because Zeb's there.

CHAPTER 10

ZEB

"GOD, WHY IS HE SUCH A DICK?" Katy says as she sucks down another sip of her sour apple martini.

I didn't hesitate to pick her up for drinks after she texted me her current "situation-ship" called it quits.

I raise my eyebrow. "He's a guy. We're dicks. It's kind of in our DNA." I shrug and take a swig of my beer.

"You're not a dick," she says candidly, and I crack a smile.

"Sure I am. Ask my exes," I reply with a sarcastic laugh.

She rolls her eyes. "That's because your exes were *boys*, Zeb. You need a *man*."

It's my turn to roll my eyes. "Yeah, tell me about it."

"I need a man, too. One that isn't afraid to fucking commit to a *serious* relationship." She frowns.

I wrap my arm around her and she leans her head on my shoulder.

"What's worse than being single and thirty?" she whines.

I crack a smile as I gaze down at her. "Being a forty-year old virgin?"

She smirks, rolling her eyes as she takes another drink.

"Shut up," she teases me.

I let out a giggle.

"Sometimes I wish I would've waited." She sighs.

"Really?" I ask.

She nods. "I don't know how the fuck he does it. I thought I was going to die if I didn't sleep with Camden junior year. I was so fucking horny."

"I remember," I quip.

"Oh, like you were any better?" She pushes me.

I give her the side eye. "Don't act all innocent over there, I know all your secrets, remember."

She puts her hand on her hip, staring me down.

I scoff, draining the last of my beer. "You calling me a manwhore, Katy Graves?"

She shrugs, giggling. "Maybe a little." She flashes her dark eyes at me.

It's my turn to push her. "And you say guys are dicks."

"I just wish I could find a guy who gets me, you know. Like you get me."

I pull her martini away.

"Hey, I didn't mean it like that..." She giggles.

"What the fuck do they put in these things?" I say. I take a sip, letting the sour apple taste settle on my tongue.

It's sweet. Too fucking sweet, and I stick my tongue out, making gagging noises.

"Not enough alcohol, that's for sure," she replies as she flags down the bartender.

"Katy..." I plead. "It's late, we should go."

"You know the drill, Z. Break ups are a three drink minimum."

I sigh as she orders us both another drink. Thank goodness we took an Uber.

"Besides, I'm on the prowl," she says confidently.

I sigh in defeat. "For you or me?"

Katy's been trying to play matchmaker for years, and while there have been guys she's introduced me to who I have liked, nothing ever really works out. For either of us. It kinda sucks.

"Tonight I'm looking for you." She flashes me with a cocky grin.

I groan. "Katy..."

"It's been, like, a year, Zeb. You need to get laid. I heard if you don't, your dick will literally fall off." She sticks her tongue out at me and I take another sip of her martini.

"Not true." I shake my head. "And didn't you just tell me you wished you *waited* longer?"

She scoffs at me with disdain. "I'm just saying, you need to get back out there," she says, turning her head to scan the room.

I know better than to argue with her when she's like this. It's pointless, so I just let her go. I'm sure she'll forget about it tomorrow.

"What about him?" She points to a guy over at the pool table. Tall, blonde, tan. Decked in flannel.

"Nope." I shake my head.

"Come on! He's cute!"

I raise an eyebrow. Yeah, he is.

I take another sip of her martini and then she grabs it from me.

"Hey!" I whine.

"What's wrong with cute?" she presses.

"I don't want cute, Katy." I sigh.

She drains the last of the neon liquid, her eyes a little glassy. Silence falls between us as she narrows her gaze at me.

"I don't want safe, or cute, or sweet. I want what's *bad* for me." The words fall out of my mouth without warning, and I feel my face flush.

Fuck, what is in this martini?

"I know." She sighs, and we both look at one another knowing the truth.

I bite my lip, breaking her gaze.

The bartender slides us both two fresh martinis.

"He's coming home in a month, you know." She flashes her gaze up at me as she pulls the cherry from her drink, holding it out to me.

I take it, popping it in my mouth, stem and all.

It takes me barely ten seconds to tie the stem in a knot. I pull it out, glancing over at the cookie cutter man in the corner, his hand running up and down his stick. He catches me looking and I turn see Katy staring at me.

"I know." I swallow hard as I take a long pull of my martini.

"You know."

The words are not a question. They are a judgment.

I pull my cherry out of my drink, sucking on the fruit to keep my damn tongue busy.

I nod.

"Keeping tabs on my brother, Z?" She smirks.

"More like your brother drunk called me the other night."

Shit.

I shouldn't have told her that.

Katy giggles, shaking her head. "I bet that was something to hear." She sips her drink.

I pull out the cherry stem, setting it on the napkin. The knot stares at me as a thicker knot forms in my stomach.

I miss you.

His voice was slow, slurred, and deep, and I can't get it out of my head, those three little drunk words.

I think about our conversations lately, and the knot in my stomach gets tighter.

"Yeah, it was... something." I nod, draining my drink.

Neither of us speaks of Geo again, and after we've both killed our martinis we catch an Uber. Our houses aren't all that far from one another.

I watch the night sky out the car window, the lights of the city passing me by as Katy rests her head on my shoulder.

"He doesn't want to come home." Her voice is barely a whisper.

"What?" I ask, my head feeling a bit hazy.

"I think he has some demons to confront," she says softly.

I purse my lips. I'm sure he does.

The Uber stops in front of my house, and Katy scoots over, letting me out of the car.

The hot air kisses my skin, and I barely register Katy telling me goodbye.

I lock the door as soon as I'm inside, wasting

no time getting undressed. It's always hot here, no matter what time of year it is.

I run a hand through my hair as I head for my bedroom. I lie back on my bed, glancing at my clock. Twelve thirty.

I queue up my phone to doomscroll, but I end up right back in my call log.

No missed calls.

He didn't call like he said he would.

I huff out a frustrated sigh, because I should have known *not* to get my hopes up.

I'd deluded myself into thinking nothing had changed between us, because just *hearing* him made me feel like everything was okay again. But it's not.

Things *are* different.

We're different.

I'm different.

I'm not the same person I was ten years ago.

I hit the number without thinking, fueled by nothing other than sour apple martinis and emotions I can't process.

"Zeb?" Geo's voice is thick with sleep, and that only pisses me off more.

"You didn't call," I snap.

I hear some moving around and Geo grunts, the sound deep, dark, and delicious.

Fucking asshole.

"You stood me up," I say, grinding my teeth.

"I just... had a lot of stuff going on," he replies, his voice smooth and tired.

I hate how his voice makes that knot in my stomach lesson.

"I'm sorry, Z," he says softly. "Are you okay? You sound—"

"Ssss... tits the fucking martinis."

Geo clears his throat. "Martinis? Like, plural?"

"Blame your fucking sister and her three drink minimum. It was her idea," I grunt.

"Oh. So you and my sister make a point of regularly getting shitfaced together, is that it?" he teases.

"Only when the men in our life fuck us over."

I realize the moment I say the words, I fucked up.

Because Geo doesn't know I'm gay, and I'm pretty sure his sister hasn't told him, because when I asked her years ago, after I came out, if she did, she told me "it's not my place to tell him, Z."

There is a heavy silence before he speaks.

"What kind of martinis?" he asks, glazing over my words.

I let out a deep breath. "Sour apple with the little fucking cherries."

Geo chuckles, and the sound is dark, smooth like silk.

"I love cherries," he says, his voice light. "They're my favorite fruit."

"Okay, maraschino cherries are not a fruit, Geo. They take, like, seven years to digest," I rattle off, and he laughs.

"Still my favorite, though."

"I know..." I snap. "Where do you think I picked up the taste for them?"

I run my hand over my face, knowing I should hang up.

I'm too drunk, and too loose-lipped.

But I can't fucking hang up. The sound of his breath, steady and slow, is like a warm hug.

I catch sight of myself in the mirror, across the room. In the amber light, I can see my reflection. My thick arms and legs, and their definition. My tan skin glistens in the low light, the dark hair covering my chest and torso standing out in contrast. My dark hair all messed up, sticking out in tufts, and the beginning of a five o'clock shadow is already starting to form on my face, despite the fact I shaved this morning.

Yet, I feel like the same tall, skinny goth nineteen-year-old I once was.

How is it that someone can change so much in ten years?

"Do you really want to see me, Geo?" I ask, and even I can hear the petulance of youth lost in my voice.

Silence blooms in its wake.

"Yes," he replies, his tone rich and deep. It threatens to pull me under.

"Do you not want to see *me*?" he asks quietly.

"Of course, I do," I whisper.

"Okay," he says softly.

For a moment, all I can hear is his heavy breathing, and then he speaks.

"Go to sleep, Z," he says as I sink down into my covers.

"Geo?" I say, my hazy alcohol-ridden brain taking over.

"Yeah?"

"You can stay with me," I suggest.

Silence beckons us again, once more the only sound his deep breathing.

"When you come home, I mean. If you don't want to stay with your parents." I clear my throat. "I mean, my house is like ten minutes away from theirs."

"You have a house?" he asks. Geo's voice is full of sadness. Guilt.

"Yeah. Bought it a couple of years ago."

"Good to know," he says softly. "Go to sleep, Z."

I curl up in my comforter, clutching the phone to my ear, and it's like all of a sudden the exhaustion is too much to fight.

"Okay," I say, letting out a tired breath. I don't hang up.

"Geo..." Sleep beckons me, but I feel like I need to say what I *need* to say, because I know when the alcohol wears off, I'll never be able to.

"Yeah?" His deep, sexy voice makes my entire body heat like a fire and I have to fight the urge to groan like a starved man lusting after the tiniest pieces of him that feel like they are meant for me.

Even if I know they aren't.

"Don't break my heart again, okay?"

"Zeb..." His voice shakes. "I—"

"Good night, G."

I hang up, and give myself to my beckoning slumber, dreaming of sweet maraschino cherries, deep sexy voices, and tattoos and ripped jeans, and I sleep like a damn baby.

GEO

HE IS DRUNK, like you were the other night.

There's no way he meant that like... that.

I let out a breath of my own as his words echo in my psyche.

Don't break my heart again.

I never wanted to break anyone's heart to begin with. My parents', my sister's, and certainly not his.

I think about his offer to let me stay with him. The only reason I didn't say yes immediately was because... well, he's drunk. I don't want to commit to something if it's not *really* what he wants, and people say stuff they don't mean all the time when they drink.

Don't break my heart again.

I try to sleep, but it's impossible, because I can't get him out of my head. His bitter tone. He was mad because I *didn't* call him.

I wanted to, but the day just... got away from me. Hours in the studio, then Kevin booked us a last minute gig on *Romano*, and by the time I actually got home, all I wanted to do was shower and go the fuck to sleep.

I toss and turn, flustered because I feel more awake than ever.

If he's up, I wonder if...

I shoot a text to my sister.

You up?

I watch as the bubbles appear instantly.

Yeah, why? Everything okay?

I shake my head, tapping out my response quick.

Heard you and Zeb had quite a night.

There is a momentary pause before she responds.

Yeah, we hang out. We always have.

I bite my lip as I contemplate asking what I want, but I feel like it's intrusive.

It could be nothing. I could be overthinking things.

I'm probably overthinking things.

But my sister has no filter when she drinks, so I know it's the most honest answer I'm going to get.

Is he...

I can't even bring myself to finish the sentence.

Why is it so hard to ask?

Why do I care?

I stare at the screen and she texts me back with a question mark.

Did he call you?

Yes.

I chew my lip, and the phone rings.

"Hey," I say.

Her voice is raspy, but there is no mistaking the shock in her voice.

"He fucking called you? What did he say?"

No greeting, no transition. Complete and utter shock.

I pull my knees up to my chest. "He was mad I didn't call him back," I say quietly.

"You guys are talking again?" she asks.

"Sort of."

Her laugh is sarcastic, but there is also a hint of shock in it as well.

"Oh, shit. No wonder he was downing those fucking martinis."

"What is that supposed to mean?" I snap.

Katy sighs. "Not my place to tell you, Geo."

What the fuck does that mean?

"He said you guys go out drinking when, and I quote 'the men in our life fuck us over'."

I don't miss the bitterness in my voice.

The jealousy.

I wish it was me throwing back sour apple martinis with him, laughing with him. But I made a choice to leave, so I know I shouldn't be jealous that Katy gets to do what I can't.

She groans dramatically. "You haven't changed a bit in the last ten years, have you, G? You still don't know."

Don't know what?

"What are you talking about, of course I've changed," I gripe.

Katy breathes out an exasperated sigh. "The fact you're calling me at one in the morning because *Zeb* got your briefs in a fucking twist asking *me* why, proves you haven't."

"He's the one who hasn't changed!" I argue. "He's the one who... who fucking called *me*—"

Katy's voice softens. "No, Geo. He's *changed*. You haven't."

"How? How has *he* changed? Tell me Katy, because I don't see it."

There is silence before she huffs out an annoyed sigh. "You really want to do this, now?" She growls, letting out a breath. "Fine."

My stomach flips as she answers me.

"For starters, he's not some lovesick teenager anymore who's scared of coming out. He's hot, twenty-nine, single as a goddamn piece of cheese, despite my intentions of *trying to* find him a decent boyfriend, and—"

"Boyfriend?" My voice cracks.

"Fuck, I didn't mean to say that." Katy curses. "Fuck, fuck, he's going to kill me."

"So he's..." I swallow harshly. I can't even say it. Because I know the second I do, it's going to change everything.

"Gay, Geo. Yeah."

"Oh." I let the words sink in.

Katy sighs again in exasperation. "Don't tell him I fucking told you, okay?" she pleads.

"Okay," I reply as I stare at my mirror, its

ghostly memories threatening to rise up with the truth of that one word.

Katy hangs up, and the line goes dead.

A flurry of guilt festers like a storm inside of me.

I should have been there for him, but I wasn't.

Katy was.

He was my best friend, and I should have been there. I should have known.

His words feel different, now, shimmering with a new context.

He's playing music again, too, Katy said.

Maybe she's right; maybe I haven't changed.

I know I should go to sleep, but I can't. Instead, I pull up Google, and I type his name in.

A couple search results pop up for local newspapers and some social media, and a YouTube.

I click on the YouTube link and it brings me to his page.

The man in the videos is not a person I recognize in the slightest.

The Zeb I remember was tall and skinny like me, with dark hair and green eyes, and an ever-present golden tan. He used to wear his dark hair across his eyes, like the other "scene" kids did; he was always sporting black eyeliner, ties, and black nail polish.

But the *man* on his YouTube looks *nothing* like that person. Except for his eyes.

Long, thick black eyelashes that make the deep, rich green of his eyes stand out against his tan skin.

His hair is still long, but doesn't hang in his eyes the same way it used to.

He's bigger, too.

Like, thicker. All around. He's shirtless in his video, his skin glistening under the light, thick dark hair decorates his chest, the guitar blocking his waist. He looks relaxed and...

Sexy as hell.

I can tell by the definition in his arms, he probably works out, but nothing crazy, and I chew on my lip as my cock jumps.

Absentmindedly I grab myself, because I can not go down this road. I fucking can't.

The video plays automatically and I can't tear my gaze away from the screen.

"Hey there, thanks for checking out my channel. If it's your first time here, hi. I'm Zeb. I play a little bit of everything, but Katy—" My sister's laugh can be heard in the background, telling him to "shut up."

"Katy thinks my covers might interest you, so let's see if she's right."

Suddenly, the voice on the phone fits the person I see. I watch as he strums his guitar, the beginning chords of a familiar pop song filling the darkness around me.

Strangers, by Kenya Grace. I recognize it because Jinger is *obsessed* with it and she's always sending me songs to listen to.

His voice is still so fucking good.

Better.

I watch his thick fingers strum the chords, noticing the way his muscles flex in his arms, his wrist as he does so. He glances up at the camera, smirking at me, and I know I'm in danger.

Oh, fuck.

His lips curve into a devilish smile as he sings about knowing someone so well, but then they fade into *strangers*.

It feels intimate. Personal. The way he sings, performs. Looks at the camera.

My cock throbs and I feel a bloom of wetness against the pad of my thumb as he croons about getting in the car and leaning over to kiss someone.

No, not someone.

A guy.

Because Zeb is gay.

He kisses *men*.

The thought, the reality should make me feel betrayed, lied to, something.

But all I can think about as I watch him, listen to his perfect voice, is how fucking hard I am.

I'm so hard it *hurts*.

I close my eyes, swallowing hard as his voice fills the room, sliding my hand over my cock, building a steady rhythm as that breathy "uh huh" uttered out of his mouth drives me over the edge into oblivion.

It doesn't take long for me to come. Not at all.

I don't even have to try this time, it just happens. Naturally.

My head falls back against the headboard and I close my eyes, groaning in blissful relief.

"Thanks for listening," he croons, his voice dark and sultry.

I open my eyes, and the guilt commences as I

catch my breath, my cock pulsing still as cum drips down my shaft.

"Don't be a stranger." He winks and then it's over.

I close my phone, reality dawning on me that I just came in my fucking pants like I was fourteen again.

Watching *him.*

The knot in my stomach returns, and I think maybe my sister's wrong.

Maybe Zeb isn't the only person who's changed.

CHAPTER 12

Zeb

I stare at Geo's number, debating if I should call him or not.

In all the years since he left, I *never* pulled a stunt like this.

Mostly because I was convinced he wouldn't even remember me, and even if he *did* have my number still, he'd take one look at it and ignore me because he was a big fucking rockstar and I was just part of his history.

Not his future.

But then I think about the phone call that started all this, and how he called me to apologize, and I reckon it's probably the right thing to do. So we're on the same page.

In a way, I guess it makes us even.

Sort of.

The phone rings once, before he picks up.

"Rough night?" His voice is edged in sarcasm and humor.

"I've had worse." I don't hide the sarcasm in my own voice.

"Is this how you became the Master of Hangovers?" he asks, and I hear a lot of crashing and thuds in the background.

Wherever he is, it's noisy as hell.

"Honestly, I'm usually pretty good at holding my liquor, really." I laugh.

"Yeah, sure, isn't that what they all say?" Geo's voice is light, energetic.

"I'm serious!" I defend my honor nobly.

"How many martinis was that again? I need to know for scientific purposes."

I shake my head, pinching the bridge of my nose, sighing deeply.

"For scientific purposes? Three." I reach for my coffee as I settle on my couch, turning on my laptop.

"Noted," he says as the background sound dies down, and I hear a door shut.

"Where are you?" I ask, curious.

"Sound check. Our tour kicks off tonight."

I blink, reality hitting me. That means...

"When, uh, when are you headed home?" I ask.

"I'll be in on the twentieth. Three weeks from today."

There is a pause before he starts to speak, then stops. I can hear the hesitation in his voice, and immediately, panic floods me.

"Everything okay?" I ask cautiously.

"Yeah. I'm fine, just... never mind."

"So, uh, Katy said you weren't dead set on a place to stay."

Geo's voice drops an octave. "I mean, I *was* going to stay at the hotel, but—"

"You can stay with me. If you want, I mean."

He lets out a breath, his voice dark and smooth, like my fucking coffee. "That depends..." he says cautiously.

"On what?" I ask.

"Do you... want me to stay? With you, I mean?"

I set my coffee down. Something about the tone of his voice feels different.

Like he means to say something else, but what, I'm not quite sure.

"I mean, I am like ten minutes down the road from your parents, and we both know you'll probably be on edge if you stay with them."

I shrug. It's the truth.

"You didn't answer my question," he says quietly.

I suck in a deep breath, knowing I'm digging my own grave.

"Of course I *want you*," I say, closing my eyes. "To stay, I mean. Do you... not want to... stay with *me*?" I try to feign nonchalance, but I fail miserably.

Geo is quick to answer. "I think I would really like to stay with you, actually."

"Really?" I ask, the surprise in my voice evident.

"Yeah, I mean, otherwise it'd just be me and my boring self back at the hotel now that everyone on the fucking label has a boyfriend, except me."

My blood chills, because his words are loud

and clear. But I know he didn't mean them like they actually sounded.

"Something in the water over at Casualty Records?" I say carefully.

"Apparently." He sighs. "You know, I'm like, totally cool with that, right?" he says.

"Cool with what?" I ask, noting he sounds shaky. Nervous.

"The... gay thing. Just saying. I'm not like my parents."

What the fuck?

Where did that come from?

Panic floods me as my eyes widen, did I...

Fuck, did I say something?

The fact I don't remember causes a fresh wave of anxiety to swell in my stomach.

"I never said you were," I reply defensively.

At first, I tried to keep my sexual confirmation on the down low, but after a year of Deb and Joel constantly trying to push me to date their daughter, I finally just had to tell them the truth, that *that* was never going to happen. They weren't thrilled with the admission, at first.

Debbie just didn't acknowledge it. Joel gave me a bit of a wide berth, at first, but he came around a lot faster than I thought he would. My own parents were actually less accepting than Geo's, to tell the truth, which is why I haven't talked to them much over the years.

"I just... needed you to know that," he says softly. "Totally cool with all of... that." And then there is a tense silence.

My cheeks flush because I know he is just saying he's supportive of his other label mates, but it feels like he's saying he's cool *with* it the... other way, but I know that's fucking impossible.

Right?

Right. Because if that were true...

"Okay..." I say casually. "Thanks for letting me know. I guess."

This conversation is making me feel like the kid who dreams he ends up naked at the talent show.

"Okay," Geo's smooth voice breathes in my ear, and it makes my stomach flip. "I'm going to be a little busy over the next few weeks, so I can't promise you I'll be able to call, but... just know, if I could, I would, okay?" I can hear the lilt in his voice.

I let out a deep breath, nodding even though he can't see me. "I get it. You're busy. You don't have to—"

"I'll call you when I can, I promise," he says, and my stupid heart threatens to beat a little faster.

"Okay. Just, uh, call me when you can, and I guess I'll see you in a couple weeks when you get in."

"Can't wait," he replies, and the excitement in his voice is genuine. The moment is short lived as I hear the crashing and thudding again.

"Gotta go, Z. See you soon."

I suck down my coffee, letting the warmth soothe my nerves.

This is really happening.

Geo's coming *home,* and he's coming *here.*

And for the first time in a long time, I think maybe the future is looking a little brighter.

CHAPTER 13

Geo

"Fuck yeah, man! We killed it!" Dare hollers, thrusting his glass of champagne up in the air.

Glasses clink, champagne spilling everywhere in the VIP suite. The last couple weeks have been a damn blur between cities. When I first signed with Casualty, I *loved* touring. Seeing all the new places, meeting new people, eating new food. Now, though, I wish there was a way to condense the time on the road between gigs.

"Yeah, we did!" Richie says, hi-fiving Dare.

Hailee downs her champagne, then her

boyfriend's, before grabbing him, leading him out to the dance floor.

It's rare that we *all* go out together like this. Felix, Mateo, *Heart Killer,* and all the bandmates in between.

Felix pushes his glass toward me.

"You look like you need this more than I do." His voice isn't judgmental or sarcastic as it usually is.

Dare downs his own champagne, wasting no time as he runs after his brother, bandmates, and Hailee, leaving me with Mateo, Felix, and Duncan. Corpse and Eddy are off somewhere; God knows where.

Probably knee-deep in pussy with Spike. Those three are like a pack of rabid wolves.

I take the glass from Felix, downing it pretty quickly.

"Thanks," I say as Mateo shifts in the booth. I catch his entertained gaze.

"What?" I ask.

"Falling off the wagon?" He smirks.

"I don't know what you're talking about," I say, clutching my glass.

He smirks, shaking his head. "I've literally known you for ten years, Geo. Seriously." He narrows his gaze at me. "This wouldn't have anything to do with your trip to Arizona, tomorrow would it?" he asks.

I watch as Duncan stretches his arms, leaning back against the booth, the edges of his fingers dancing along Felix's leather jacket.

I was just as surprised as the rest of the world when they both waltzed on *Romano* holding holds and announced they were dating.

I mean, Felix is... well, Felix. Sure, there were rumors about him and his former bandmate, but I learned pretty fast in this business not everything you read or hear is true.

Still, if you would have told me that the four-time Grammy winner was gay, I would never have believed it had I not seen him making out with Duncan backstage the night of our LA show, and well, pretty much *every* show since.

"Just, uh, nervous I guess. Haven't been home in a long time."

"How long has it been?" Duncan asks.

Felix leans back into his space, looking up at him.

"Ten years," I mumble.

Duncan raises an eyebrow. "Ten years sounds like you're avoiding the place."

Mateo sips his champagne knowingly. "Or someone who lives there."

"It's... complicated." I pour myself another drink.

Duncan sighs. "Yeah, usually is."

My head starts to feel hazy, and I think the champagne is finally kicking in. The song that comes over the speakers stops me mid-pour.

Strangers, by Kenya Grace.

I glance at Mateo, who's casually watching Dare, a soft smile on his face as Dare dances among the crowd, then flash my gaze to Felix, who is casually resting against Duncan's chest as he focuses on his phone as those breathy "uh huh's" sound out over the speakers, reminding me of someone else.

His cover is so much better.

The words fall out of my mouth without warning.

"How did you know?" I ask, blinking.

Mateo turns to me. "Know what?" he asks, and takes a drink of his champagne.

"That you were gay?" I word-vomit the words, immediately regretting it.

Felix laughs.

He fucking laughs.

"Shit, Graves, we gotta get you loaded more often."

Mateo shoots him a scathing look. "Shut up, asshole."

Felix shakes his head as Duncan gives him a shove.

"Forget I said anything—" I can feel my cheeks flushing as I move to get up, but Mateo stops me.

"Sit the fuck down." He points to Felix. "You, shut the fuck up." His voice is commanding, stern, and it's hard to refute.

I sit my ass back down, but I don't look at him.

Felix flicks him off. "Fuck you, *Matty.*"

Mateo ignores him.

"Why do you ask?" he says, imploring me with his gaze. It's not judgmental. Not in the least bit. "You having a mid-life gay awakening or something?"

"No!" I bark, but my voice is a little too high for my own liking. "I'm just... uh... testing a new demographic.".

Felix laughs. "How old is your *demographic*?" he taunts.

"Twenty-nine."

Mateo grins. "That's older than Felix."

Felix flicks him off again. "Fuck you, cradle robber. Least I'm older than your golden retriever."

"Both of you shut the fuck up," Duncan grunts, and I hang my head in my hands.

This was a terrible idea. Fucking champagne.

I must make a mental note to tell Zeb I cannot drink champagne. Ever.

"I asked my kid how he knew he was gay and you know what he told me?"

I look up at him, my jaw tense. "What?"

"He asked me how I knew I was *straight.* And I couldn't say with absolute certainty that I was."

I blink as his words settle. "But you were married, right?"

Duncan nods. "Yup. A lot of wonderful years."

He looks at Felix, his smile lighting up the corners of his eyes, and then he says, "Porn."

Felix frowns. "What?"

"Was trying to convince myself I *wasn't* into you. Failed miserably."

Felix laughs, and it is deep, genuine. Happy.

"Brad Drexler," Mateo says, shaking his head. "Ninth grade. We used to masturbate together."

I wrinkle my nose and he laughs.

Felix huffs with annoyance. "Not that it's *anyone's* business, but..." He flicks his blonde hair over his shoulder, flashing me a stone cold blue gaze. "Nick Rialoto," he says seriously. "He told me to suck him off and I didn't think twice about it." He shrugs. "Pretty sure I was, like, sixteen."

I think I need another glass of champagne.

"Does the demographic live in Arizona?" Felix pushes the bottle toward me, but Mateo pushes it aside.

"Do you *like* the demographic?" Mateo asks.

"Yes, and I don't know," I answer honestly. "I've been pretty set on one demographic for a long time, you know."

Duncan lets out a chuckle.

"I know," Mateo says. "Maybe you need to do some research." He grins.

"Research?" I ask, trying to process his words as Dare barrels into the booth, dropping himself into Mateo's lap, which pushes me aside a bit.

He laughs freely, grabbing Mateo by the jaw and kisses him.

Two fucking inches from my face.

"Gross, get a fucking room!" Felix growls as he throws a garnish of some sort at Dare's head. The flash of pink bops Dare in the head, bouncing back into my lap.

I pick it up.

It's a fucking maraschino cherry.

I look from the cherry to the couple before me.

Mateo lightly shoves Dare off of his lap, running his thumb over his lip. He winks at me. "Research."

"What are we researching?" Dare asks as Mateo pours him a drink.

"Nothing," he says.

I let out a nervous laugh.

Felix pulls my attention when he speaks. "Good luck with your demographic, Geo," he says as he gets up. "I'm fucking beat. I'll see you idiots tomorrow."

Mateo flicks him off, as Duncan chuckles, heading after Felix.

"Thanks," I say as I climb to my feet. "I think I should probably call it a night, too.

Mateo nods. "You know my trailer's always open right?" he says, chewing his bottom lip. "If you have questions about branching out into new *demographics.*" He flashes me a smile. "Or if you just need to talk."

I nod, feeling a fraction better. "I'll remember that, thanks."

I sit on my tour bus, staring at the Google search engine, my fingers steepled in front of my mouth.

The cursor flashes, and I glance ahead at Clarence, my driver.

I can see the top of his head through the sliver of partition that separates the back of the bus from the front driver's console.

Most of the guys, except for Mateo, Hailee, and Felix, share their tour bus space. *Heart Killer* has their own bus, technically, but Dare's been bunking with Mateo, just like Duncan and Felix have been sharing a bus, and Richie's been bunking with Hailee. The rest of *Heart Killer* and Felix's band have been sharing a bus, and me... well, technically, I don't have a regular band. I never have.

Usually, when I tour on my own, we get local

musicians to play backup, but the *Pillars Of Rock* tour has *Heart Killer* backing me up since I'm on after them, anyway.

So once again, it's just me. All by my fucking self. Which, for what I'm considering to do, is definitely a blessing right now.

I glance at Clarence, then back to my screen.

I feel like a fucking criminal as I slowly type *porn* into the search bar.

Like at any minute my mother's going to show up and ground me, or someone's going to fall through the fucking roof and shout my sins across all of social media.

I know I'm an adult, and it's not that weird, but old habits die hard.

"You're not doing anything *wrong*," I mumble to myself. "Pretty sure you are the one percent who is the weirdo because you *don't* look at porn."

My reflection in the screen warps as I shift in my bed, letting out a deep breath.

I hover over the "get lucky" button.

Duncan said he looked up porn to try and convince himself he wasn't into Felix. And it inadvertently ended up confirming that he was, indeed, bisexual.

So I think it sounds like a viable way to determine if I'm indeed having a "mid-life gay awakening" as Mateo called it.

Could I be bisexual?

I'm not sure. I mean, I don't really have a *ton* of experience with women, but I do have *some.*

I've kissed a lot of girls, which was okay.

That has to count for something right?

I've finger-fucked two, which wasn't a terrible experience either time, but it was really wet and warm and squishy. I didn't *dislike* how my girlfriends responded to my touch, but I wasn't entirely sure they weren't faking it, either, and I didn't want to ask. And even though I felt pressured, I have had my cock sucked once—by Tiffany. Though, I immediately regretted *that* experience.

It felt good at first, and I wanted to come, if only because I knew I *should*, but I couldn't. Getting there was... well, I never got there.

Because I felt guilty as hell.

I'm pretty sure she took it personally, which made things worse, and I couldn't fake that I didn't like her teeth scraping against my skin or that her grip on my balls wasn't as pleasurable as I thought it was going to be.

To be honest, it kind of hurt and the whole thing just kind of backfired and confirmed maybe it was better that I remained just... not. Until I met the right person, of course, but I'm starting to think I'm just going to be this way *forever.*

I glance back at the screen as sadness blooms in the pit of my stomach, my reflection warped.

I don't want to be like this forever, though.

I don't want to be alone, relegated to fantasies in my head that make me feel guilty.

I want to experience the things I sing about —romance, love, sex. I don't want to second guess myself, or feel inadequate. I want to fall in love, I want to be touched, and feel all those sparks and flames.

I want someone to fall into my lap and kiss me until I can't fucking breathe, and I want to fucking lose my virginity before I die.

I want answers, God damn it!

I delete the word porn, shaking my head. "This is a terrible idea," I mutter.

I type "gay porn" into the search bar, sucking in a deep breath. "Even worse idea." I click my tongue. Cross my arms.

"It's just… research," I try to convince myself. "It's a test."

I bite my bottom lip.

I hit search.

The results are… interesting. Everything from Only Fans to Porn Hub, to some Tumblr titled *malesmasturbating*.

I close my eyes and blindly pick a link. When I open my eyes, I see video of a tall, slender man and a woman kissing.

So far, so good, I guess.

"Completely normal. Everyone does this."

I watch as they kiss, their hands exploring, and then she tells him she'll be back later as his friend arrives to watch the game.

It seems innocent enough, and the actors are attractive, so I get comfortable. The guys seem comfortable with one another, laughing, hanging out on the couch watching sports together.

Then the friend sets his hand on the boyfriend's leg. The camera shows his hand, squeezing, rubbing up and down his subject's leg. I watch in interest and horror as the mood shifts, the friend *grabs* the boyfriend's cock through his jeans and my own jumps.

I bite my lip, every nerve in my body standing at attention.

But I can't stop watching.

The boyfriend looks back at his friend with pleading eyes.

"Tell me you don't want this," the friend says.

Boyfriend grabs his friend by the neck and I take stock of the way his fingers grip his neck.

"Please, put me out of my misery," he begs.

I watch as his fingers grip his friend's hair.

Boyfriend keeps one hand on his friend's neck while his other hand frees his own cock.

My breath catches in my throat, and I stare as he *shoves* the friend's face against his gleaming cock.

"Tell me *you* don't want to choke on this dick."

I slide my hand beneath my pajama pants, noting my hardness, and the relief is instant.

I swallow harshly as I watch the friend swallow down Boyfriend's cock like it's a damn popsicle, and that does it.

It's like a switch has flipped somewhere inside of me.

I shut the laptop as tears threaten to pool in my eyes.

I failed.

I fucking failed the test.

God, help me.

"Fuck," I curse as I look out the window.

Does this mean I'm fucking gay?

I pull my hand away from my hardness, sucking in a deep breath.

The silence is deafening as I am overcome with loneliness, confusion, and guilt.

So much fucking *guilt.*

My phone chirps, and I glance at it to see the notification.

It's Zeb.

I grab my phone, trying to quiet my guilty sobs the best I can.

You up?

I debate answering him because it feels like if I do, I'm crossing some invisible line that he doesn't even know about.

But I do it anyway, because it feels better than the alternative of crying alone on my tour bus over my first experience with porn and a potential mid-life gay awakening.

Fuck.

Yeah. Can't sleep.

Zeb texts back instantly. *Me either.*

A soft smile tugs at my mouth, but my eyes are still blurry.

What time are you getting in tomorrow?

I ease back into my bed as I text him back. *Ten-thirty.*

My stomach flips, my nerves fraying.

It's been *ten years.* And in *ten hours* ten years will disappear.

CHAPTER 14

Zeb

Today is the day.

I stare at the road, Fall Out Boy's *Dead on Arrival* blaring through my speakers. The hot Arizona air filters through my windows as I try my hardest not to overthink things.

I don't miss the irony of Patrick Stump telling me this conversation is dead on arrival, but I don't bother changing the station, because at least the emo station doesn't play *Gravedigger*, and I know if I'm going to make it through the next week with the Graves, I need to have as clear a head as possible.

What better way to clear my head than to jam out to my favorite songs, right?

When I get to the Morningstar Hotel, I pull up to the gated parking area like Geo told me to do last night. There's a small group of fans collected out front, and I watch as security ushers them around, dispelling them so I can make it through.

The attendant takes one look at me and my red pickup truck and raises an eyebrow, but he just hands me a ticket and says, "To the left. The buses are starting to arrive."

I flash him my best smile as I pull through the open gate, turning left. Sure enough, I come to a gigantic lot that is already starting to fill up with other cars, and then I see a bus turn in.

I glance at my clock, noting it's only ten-fifteen.

I park, but I don't turn the music off, because honestly, it's the only thing keeping me from jumping out of my fucking skin right now.

If you would have told me a month ago that I'd be picking Geo Graves up from his hotel and catching up while he was in town, I would not have believed you.

I'm not stupid, and I know this is probably a

bad idea, if only because the desire to fall back into old roles is really tempting, but I also feel like maybe, just maybe, I need this.

Katy's right. I do need to put myself back out there, but maybe I need to confront *my demon* first before I do it. Or, more accurately, the man who altered my fucking DNA.

I tap my fingers along to Dashboard Confessional's *Vindicated*, watching as the buses file in.

I get out of the car, leaning against the front of my truck, arms crossed. I watch them empty, noting who comes out of what bus.

I know I should probably feel star struck, because standing in front of me are some of the biggest acts on the rock scene today. Felix Hart, *Heart Killer*, Mateo Starr from *Mage Of Mercy*.

My jaw tenses.

Up until recently, my Geo Graves detox meant I wasn't looking *him* up, but it's honestly impossible sometimes to avoid news about a celebrity.

And Mateo Starr was *always* a hot topic on social media, especially since his public break up, and as of late, his whirlwind romance with up-and-coming *Heart Killer* frontman, Dare Wylde.

I shouldn't be jealous of the man, I know that, but I can't help it.

Geo and Mateo's "bromance" has been documented well enough over the years, and I've certainly seen the evidence a time or two, even though I tried to avoid it.

Playing shows together, going out to clubs. Doing everything *I* should have been doing with him.

Mateo stops, looking up and catching my gaze. Dare Wylde jumps out of the bus next to him, pulling his attention, and then I see him.

The last bus unloads, and it's like time stops.

Geo steps down and onto the pavement, his dark hair blowing in the wind like in those dumb, cheesy romance movies.

He doesn't see me; instead, he nods at Mateo, and I frown.

Mateo cocks his head, and then Geo turns to look at me, and...

The smile that forms on his face is absolute perfection and melts all the tension away.

I push off of my car, taking one step, then two, then three.

Geo slides one hand in his pocket while the other pulls a rolling suitcase, his guitar slung over his back, grinning like a damn kid as he picks up his pace, and before I know it he's in front of me.

"Hey," he says, pulling me into a tight hug.

I startle for a moment, because I wasn't expecting a hug.

A handshake, maybe, but a *hug*...

My entire body sinks into him like ink into paper, and instinctively, I wrap my arms around him, burying my face in his shoulder.

He smells exactly the same as I remember. Like orange blossoms and spicy cedar. Like a core memory.

His fingers grip my shoulder and I feel him relax instantly.

Whoever said hugs are the best medicine, wasn't fucking kidding.

I break away, if only because I know if I don't we'll never make it to my truck, and it's still running.

"Hey," I reply, grinning with excitement.

He brushes some dark hair out of his eyes, and I reach for his suitcase.

"Oh, you don't have to—"

"Don't worry about it." I turn to see Mateo staring at me like I'm a science experiment.

"What's his problem?" I ask as I stroll toward my car.

"Who? Mateo?" Geo asks. "Nothing. He just suggested we all should get together and hang out."

"Who's we?" I ask as I toss Geo's luggage in the back bed.

"Like, my friends. You know, the guys... Felix, Duncan, Dare, Hailee, Richie..." He rattles their names off so comfortably. "You."

I shoot him a raised eyebrow. "Your famous *friends* know about me?"

Geo shrugs. "Why wouldn't they? You are my... friend, right?"

I don't know why that thought or his question bothers me, but it does.

What exactly has he *said* about me?

I relax slightly. "Yeah." I nod, even though I'm not entirely sure *friend* is the right word.

Sure, once we were friends. But the word doesn't feel like it fits now, though I'm not sure what I'd really define us as.

"Of course we're friends." I smile. "No reason, I guess," I say as I open the door for him.

His amber eyes glance up at me, and I realize I'm actually a little taller than him now.

Not by much, but it's noticeable. Ten years ago, I looked up at him.

"Thanks," he says as he climbs in the passenger side, and I don't miss the way his shirt slides up his sides, showing off those dark, black lines of ink that dip below his waistband.

I pretend I don't notice, but my cock definitely notices.

When I get to the driver's side, I notice he's staring at me.

"What?" I ask as I climb into my seat and turn the key, the vehicle roaring to life and then settling into a deep rumble.

Geo pulls some shades out from his front pocket of his burgundy shirt.

"You just... you look good, Z," he says casually. "Different, but good."

I watch as he puts them on, the way the sun glints off of the silver arms.

I don't know what to say, so I say nothing.

I drive us back through the gate, handing my pass to the attendant, who once again raises his eyebrow but says nothing.

I let out a breath that the group of fans seems to have dispersed, and it doesn't take us long to get back on the road.

"Hope your drive wasn't too bad," he says, leaning back in my passenger seat. His spicy citrus-woodsy scent fills my car and I have to fight the desire to sigh.

"Not at all," I reply, shooting him a genuine smile.

The beginning chords of Boys Like Girl's *Great Escape* fill the space as I lean my arm out the window. Geo does the same.

"Oh, shit, I'm sorry, you can change if it you want," I say, noticing how he is glancing at the radio.

"Driver picks the music, remember?" he says with a smirk. "Besides, I haven't heard these guys in forever." He's tapping his fingers against the edge of the windowsill, keeping time with the beats of the song.

And then he *sings,* and I feel like I really am nineteen again.

He belts out those high notes, crooning on about making a great escape, and I don't even think about singing along with him, like we used to.

Geo starts to bounce a bit, the rhythm alive in his voice and in the space between us.

His energy is contagious.

And before I know it, we're both singing at the top of our fucking lungs to every song that comes on the whole way home.

When we finally get back to my place, my face hurts from smiling so damn much.

Maybe this won't be so bad after all.

I grab his luggage from the car.

He stands on my sidewalk, his pale arms contrasting the black tank he's wearing.

I come up next to him, noticing the way he looks at my house, and I feel a sense of pride.

"I know it's no Morningstar, but there's WiFi," I tease.

Geo glances at me. "It's perfect, Z. It's you."

"Okay, so I'll give you the quick tour, and then we can grab lunch? Or if you just want to hang out, rest, we can—"

"Lunch is good." Geo nods, slowly sauntering over to my kitchen island.

I freeze, watching the way the light from the kitchen shines through the windows, hitting the suncatchers that bathe him in rainbows and sparkles.

It's hard to believe the man in front of me is the same person I fell in love with ten years ago.

But that spark that refuses to listen beckons to my foolish heart.

"So yeah, kitchen—" I twirl around my small kitchen, then point to the left. "Living room, sun room—"

I motion for him to follow me down the hall, and he doesn't hesitate.

"Bathroom, my bedroom—" I say the words quickly, dragging his luggage to the last room, across from my mine.

"Guest room slash music room. Figured you'd probably like this better than the couch." I mumble the last bit, feeling an influx of sudden warmth. I drop his luggage off in the doorway of the guestroom.

He slides up to the doorframe, peeking in. He braces his arms on both sides, the motion drawing attention to the prominent muscles in his broad shoulders and back.

The definition looks good on him.

"It's nice. Cozy," he says, walking into the room.

I slide my hands in my pockets, adjusting my stupid cock.

My phone is chirping away as it vibrates in

my back pocket. I know it's Katy, but I don't have the wherewithal to text her right now.

I just want to hold on to this moment, watching Geo in *my house* a little longer before everything goes up in flames. Because I know as soon the Graves family enters the chat, shit's going to hit the fan.

Geo jumps on the bed, his head hitting the pillows. He spreads his arms out along both sides, moaning out a sigh of relief.

"Oh, this is nice…" he says, closing his eyes.

I enter the room slowly, leaning against the dresser. "If you'd rather rest, you can—"

Geo leans up on his elbows, and the sight of him here, like this—dark hair falling in his eyes, positioned the way he is—I know I need to keep my distance.

"I'll sleep when I'm dead," he says as he pushes himself up. He casually strolls over to where I'm standing, leaning one arm out to brace himself against the dresser. His dark gaze catches mine and I have to focus on *breathing*.

This is really happening.

Geo's in my fucking house.

My phone rings and Geo gaze's flashes to my side. "You going to get that?"

"It can wait," I say with a shrug.

Geo's phone rings, and I can't help but roll my eyes as the text messages chirp one after the other in rapid succession.

"You going to get that?" I ask. I watch as he silences his phone, a grin forming on my face.

"Nope. It can wait." He smirks.

I nod. "Okay, then. I'm starving, how about you?"

CHAPTER 15

Geo

The minute I saw Zebulon Ingram standing in front of his red pickup truck, all dark features and glistening golden skin, reality hit me like a sledgehammer.

Mateo nudged my shoulder. "New demographic?"

I nearly choked on my own words, because suddenly, I found it hard to speak.

"Uh huh," I said as Mateo chuckled.

"You should go."

"I should go," I repeated, blinking as I came back to the here and now.

"We should all hang out later," he called out, and I nodded in response, feeling both flustered and overwhelmed at the idea of my past and my present colliding.

Not that I think the guys would be shitty or anything, in fact, I'm pretty sure, given their advice and their support, they'd be all over Zeb if I brought him around.

Which somehow only makes me feel more vulnerable, more anxious.

Maybe it's just best if I keep him to myself a little while until I get a grip on this whole new demographic thing.

My parents aren't exactly anti-queer or anything, but it was heavily implied that same-sex relationships were not seen in the same way traditional relationships were in our house. I often wondered what my parents would have said if I came home one day and said "I'm gay!", but when I thought about it then, it was more or less teenage angst over the control my mother kept over me.

Then, it was a question of, "what if" in the sense that I thought at times, I'd do *anything* to get away from my parents because I felt like they were suffocating me with their idealistic image they felt God wanted me to represent.

But now...

Now it's like for the first time I'm seeing everything from an entirely new perspective.

Including the sinfully attractive man who's taken the place of the young adult I once knew.

The entire ride home, I couldn't stop gawking at him while we sang along to all the songs we loved. Even though I'd seen his photos, watched his YouTube videos, even though I knew what I was walking into, I don't think anything could have prepared me for how it felt to see him again. To hug him.

Once, we were like peanut butter and jelly. We just... worked. Despite the age difference between us, Zeb got me, and he accepted me for who I was, and that was mutual. It really was the easiest friendship I'd ever had.

Back then, I wouldn't have thought twice about hugging him, because we were just close and he was like a part of the family.

But now...

God strike me down, I didn't want to let go of him. I liked how it felt in a way that I know can't be classified as friendly.

His hold was tight, warm, and even if he didn't look the same, the familiarity was there in the way he smelled; like vetiver and tonka beans mixed with teakwood.

He smelled like home, and I just wanted to close my eyes and dig my fucking grave in those much larger, golden arms.

It wasn't awkward, at all, like I thought it would be, and it soothed something fractured inside of me, while at the same time, it felt like some invisible wall within me and around us had crumbled.

We sang the entire way home, to his house, and for the first time in a long time, I felt like *me*.

I'd watched him intently as he led me around his house, trying to picture what the last ten years had been like for *him*. Because for me, they were so fucking *lonely*.

Sure, I released five albums, toured the world with *Mage Of Mercy* twice, and won a slew of awards, but at the end of the day, it was just *me*.

When you're chasing your dreams, trying to build the life you so desperately want, you never realize that you're missing out on life as it's happening. Not until you cross your threshold into nothing but silence, or crawl into bed alone knowing you sacrificed every-thing for it.

Katy never talked about Zeb when I called her, and I never asked about him, either. It was sort of an unspoken rule, because my sister knows more than anyone how badly I regret how things panned out when I left.

My decision to leave was the hardest decision I ever made, but I knew it was the right one at the time.

But I'll always feel some deep remorse over it, knowing I burned some bridges in the process.

At least, I thought I had, but now...

Now, as I stand in Zeb's guest bedroom, inches away from him, I have to wonder if perhaps some bridges are capable of being repaired.

Or perhaps, renovated into something new.

Something better.

I've never been the best when it comes to relationships in general. Most of my girlfriends were of the outgoing, bubbly, and confident vari-ety, which was a blessing because it meant that they were also the type to pursue *me*.

And as a sex-starved twenty-something who felt stifled by his overprotective, image obsessed

Christian parents, I think I would have said yes to just about anyone at the time even if they walked up to me out of nowhere and said, "Hey, you're cute, Geo Graves! You're my boyfriend now!"

Desperate people do desperate things, right?

I know Mateo is right, I *do* need to do my research. To know for sure.

I mean, watching porn once, for the first time in general, might skew my results, right?

Except, I know I have more evidence than just the one video.

I've got my fantasies, and those have only gotten more intense over the weeks, even before I watched the porn.

And I'd be lying if I said I didn't enjoy it because it feels really fucking good all of a sudden. Like, I actually *enjoy it.*

And there's also the thick tension and the lump in my throat when I looked at Zeb in the guest bedroom and realized he was close enough to fucking *kiss.*

Thank the lord my sister texted me.

I'm slightly afraid of what might have happened if she didn't.

A hundred emotions and thoughts filter through my brain as I try to process everything.

Do I *want* to kiss him?

I think about Duncan's admission from the other night, and the fact I can't say no, makes me feel a certain sense of nervousness that is on par with the guilt I *used* to feel when I used to pleasure myself. Sure, I still feel some guilt when I masturbate now, but that guilt is more or less because I am slightly worried I'm forming an unhealthy attachment to my cock now that getting to the finish line is easier, than it is about what I'm thinking about while I'm doing it.

I can't say with full certainty, no, I don't want kiss him.

But I'm not going to assume just because he's gay, he'd want to kiss me either, even if it's just to... you know... help me figure this out.

That sounds selfish, right?

I'm not even sure if or how I want to approach the topic with him.

Would he do it?

For scientific purposes?

Would I like it if he did?

Shit, what if *I* like it and he doesn't?

What if I'm a terrible kisser?

That'd be super fucking awkward.

My girlfriends never said I was bad, but they never said I was good, either.

I decide to stuff the raging mid-life crisis thoughts down as he parks the car at *Carl's Cantina.*

I didn't even notice that we'd arrived, too tied up in my own insanity, I guess.

Zeb shoots me a glance. "You okay?"

I unbuckle my seat belt, heading for the door. "Yeah, of course. Just, uh... kind of dissociated there for a bit."

Zeb climbs out, jogging around the vehicle and opening my door before I can, and I look at him where he stands. I step down and he slams the door shut.

Thankfully, my sunglasses and hat keep me somewhat incognito enough that I don't think we'll be bothered too much, which I'm thankful for.

After last night's shenanigans and today's myriad of confusing thoughts and emotions, I am more than ready to eat my feelings.

The host sits us down quickly, and I don't hesitate to pull up a chair, burying my head in the menu.

"What can I get you boys to drink?" Our

waitress asks, and I don't miss the way she bats her eyelashes at Zeb. I feel a pang of jealousy that I know is totally unfounded. To his credit, he doesn't even blink.

But it strikes me like lightning, nonetheless.

"Probably just a beer and a water," he says nodding to me. "What about you?"

I take one look at him, then the bar. "You have sour apple martinis?" I ask. "With the little cherries?"

The waitress smiles. "Absolutely, sugar."

I nod with a grin. "I'll take one of those, please."

I don't miss the way Zeb shakes his head.

"What?" I ask innocently. "I want to see what all the fuss is about."

"Really?" He laughs and I shrug as the waitress heads to grab our drinks.

Across the room, I see a couple patrons socializing. A man and a woman in the corner taking selfies, another couple sharing a plate of nachos, and in the far left corner.

"So, uh... you come here often?" I attempt to make conversation, even though I know I'm terrible at it.

"Not as often as I like for leisure. But I play here a lot."

"Yeah, Katy said you were kind of a big deal around these parts," I say.

I don't miss the way his eyes glisten with excitement. "Really? She said that?"

Okay, so I *may* have Googled him a bit more.

Okay, maybe more than a bit, but I don't need to tell him that because then he might actually think I *am* a pervy, creepy, old man.

And I really don't want him to think I'm any of those things.

"Yeah. I, uh, saw some of your recent stuff. On your YouTube page," I offer as our waitress sets down our drinks.

Zeb chews his bottom lip as he reaches for his beer. The waitress takes our orders, and it takes entirely too long for my liking.

But once she's gone, I take a sip of my martini, puckering my lips from the tart taste.

It's like drinking a cold, liquid version of a jolly rancher.

But I kind of like it.

"Yeah. You sound great, really," I say as I let the sour concoction coat my throat.

"Yeah? You think so?" he asks, smiling from ear to ear.

"I mean, you always sounded great to me. Even back then." I spin my cherry around the green potion by its stem. "But now..." I let my voice trail off as I take another sip of my drink.

"Now, what?" he asks. He shifts in his seat, which draws his stool a little closer to me.

I look up at him, at his bright green eyes, the way his dark hair falls across his temple. The way he twists his lush, full lips.

"Now, it fits. The deep, sexy voice, I mean." I feel a flush creep up my cheeks the minute I say it, and I turn in my seat if only to avoid the look on his face, because I suddenly feel like a baby bird that's been dropped out of their nest.

"So you think my voice is sexy, huh?" He chuckles, nudging me with his shoulder.

I turn to look at him, realizing he's gotten closer. "Yeah. It suits you. And your music, of course."

"Mhmm." He raises an eyebrow. *Is he... is he flirting with me?*

"So, uh, besides singing sexy covers on Youtube, uh, what else have you been up to?" I ask, running a hand through my hair.

God, I suck at this small talk shit.

Zeb shrugs. "Not much, really. Just the music, mostly."

"Drinking with my sister."

Zeb laughs, shaking his head. "Yeah, that, too."

I take another sip of my martini.

"So are you, like, seeing… anyone?" I throw out carefully. "Or, you know, in the last ten years, in general?"

Zeb cocks his head to the side. "There were a few people, but uh, nothing serious." He pauses, his beer halfway to his lips. "You?" he asks.

I purse my lips. "There were a few women, but, uh… nothing serious." I let out a frustrated sigh.

"Still waiting?" he asks, his gaze dipping to the warm steel band around my ring finger, and I feel the weight of his question in a way that is terrifying and new.

"For the right woman, I mean?" He chokes a little on his beer, smacking his chest to clear it.

"Just waiting for the right *demographic*, I guess." I shift my weight in the chair, feeling strangely on the spot.

He narrows his gaze. "What?"

"Never mind," I say, shaking my head.

I look at my martini, and immediately, I regret my decision to drink this damn thing because the words that come out of my mouth next are completely beyond my brain's control.

"How come you never told me you were gay?" I say, fixating my gaze on him.

I watch his smile fade, his eyes darken.

"It was an accident. Katy—"

Zeb's jaw tenses, and immediately, I reach out, setting my hand on his arm. His gaze flashes to mine.

"It just sort of came out the other night after the sour apple martinis, and I just—"

I let out a breath as I watch Zeb's jaw tense, his eyebrows furrow.

Fuck!

"Somehow I am not surprised," he says, letting out a breath, shaking his head slightly.

"Hey, I told you I'm cool with it. I just—"

"You just what?" he says, his voice thick with panic.

I know panic better than anyone.

I squeeze his arm, imploring him with my gaze. "I just... thought we were close, you know. I thought... I thought you would have told me something like that."

Zeb stares at my hand where it rests, then he glances up at me. "I didn't think you wanted to know," he says, his voice serious.

"Zeb..."

He slides his arm from underneath me.

"When?" I ask softly.

"Three years after you left."

The temporary stitch unravels itself in my heart.

"You could have called me, you know," I say.

Zeb takes a swig of his beer. "What was I gonna say, Geo?" His voice is thick with emotion and I watch the way he rubs his arm, his large hand settling where mine was only a minute ago.

The desire to reach out and touch him is overwhelming.

To make him feel better, to make him understand I'm not angry with him.

I just feel like I should have been there for him.

But I can be there for him now, right?

"You could have called me, too, you know," he says gruffly.

It's my turn to sigh deeply and I take another sip of my martini, swallowing hard.

"I didn't think you wanted anything to do with me," I admit.

Zeb sighs. "I didn't."

I look down at my hands, gripping my drink.

"But I still wanted to hear my friend's voice all the same," he says, his voice barely a whisper.

The waitress drops off our food, and I let out a sigh of relief.

I look at Zeb as he squeezes a lime on his tacos, and I feel the weight of the world on my shoulders.

"I'm sorry," I say, and he stops.

His lips turn up in the slightest ghost of a smile. "I know. I'm sorry, too," he replies.

There is a solid silence between us, and I take a bite of my burger, relishing in the tart sauce and pickles for the moment.

"What happened in the past, it's... it's in the past, right?" he says quietly, drawing my attention.

I lick my lips as I look at his deep, green eyes. The way his eyebrows furrow.

"You're here now."

He passes me the hot sauce for my fries

without my asking, and my heart lifts a little. It feels like an olive branch, but it also feels like so much more.

"I'm here now," I agree, my heart in my throat.

He gives me a soft smile, and the stitch starts to repair itself again.

"So, make it up to me now."

I THINK a lot about Zeb's words as we head back to his place to shower and get ready to meet my parents and my sister for dinner and cocktails.

Thank God there will be alcohol, because I'm not sure I'd be able to do this sit down family dinner with my parents without it, given that the day's already been pretty emotionally taxing.

I glance at Zeb, noting the way his dark hair blows in the wind, his facial hair stark against his pronounced, tanned jaw, the length of his thick lashes, set against the desert sky.

So make it up to me now.

God, where do I start?

My phone goes off, and I see that it's Mateo.

How's your research going?

I glance at Zeb, tapping out my reply as The Used's *I Caught Fire* blares through the speakers.

It's complicated.

Mateo texts me back quickly.

No, it isn't. You're just overthinking it.

I huff out an aggravated sigh. Easy for him to say.

Zeb casts me a look. "Who's that?"

"Mateo."

I don't miss the way Zeb's hand grips the steering wheel or the way his jaw sets.

What does he have against Mateo?

Mateo texts me back.

I don't know how to do any of this, Mateo. Literally any of it.

"What's he want?" Zeb asks.

"Just checking to see how things are going," I say. It's not a complete lie.

"You guys are pretty close, I take it?" he asks smoothly.

I shift uncomfortably in my seat. "Yeah, I guess he's kinda like the closest thing I have to a best friend in the biz." I shrug. "We've been on tour a couple of times together."

Zeb grips the steering wheel as my phone chirps. I look down at the screen.

Dare says you should do "the lean."

What the fuck is the *lean*? I text him a question mark.

When you're alone, feeling comfortable, lean into his space. If he leans in, too, it's a pretty good indicator he probably wants you to kiss him.

My cheeks heat and I slam my phone down in my lap, turning to look out the window.

The reality of what we're talking about hits like a thousand bricks.

"What's he saying?" Zeb asks as he stops at a red light.

"Nothing." I glance back at Zeb, who is raising an eyebrow at me, and I feel my phone vibrate against my cock. Which clearly has a mind of its own.

"Doesn't look like nothing," he replies.

"Just the usual bullshit." I force a smile.

Zeb nods slowly. "Okay."

Once he takes off again, I look at my phone.

Dare says you got this.

I chew my bottom lip, hoping he's right.

CHAPTER 16

ZEB

"I'LL BE FAST, PROMISE," Geo says as he heads for the bathroom.

I nod. "I mean, we don't have to be at your parents until six, and they are ten minutes down the road, so we've got plenty of time," I reply as I head for my bedroom to grab my change of clothes.

Geo leans in the doorway, clutching his towel and a makeup bag full of "his face", as he says, to his chest.

Set against the pale blue of my bathroom, he looks like the fucking Grim Reaper.

"Right, of course. I'm, uh... going to shower now," he says, blinking before turning around and closing the door.

He's been acting weird all afternoon, but I guess I can't blame him after our conversation at lunch.

Granted, I knew it needed to happen, and I'm glad it's out of the way now, but I'm still a little pissed about Katy just letting things slip because she was always adamant it wasn't her place.

But in a way, I'm also kind glad she gave me an out, too.

I get undressed, tossing my shirt and jeans in the hamper, as I set about to finding my outfit for dinner.

Growing up, I spent a lot of time over at the Graves', even before I started working for them as Geo's guitarist.

Family dinners aren't black tie or anything, but Debbie and Joel insist that everyone be in their Sunday best when they do have family dinner. Especially if guests are in from out of town.

I set out a purple button down with shimmery monstera fern motifs and a pair of black dress pants, just as the bathroom door opens. I head for the hallway to grab my towel, and then I run smack into Geo.

"Shit, sorry. I forgot my fa—"

I settle my hands on his biceps without thinking, and his voice disappears.

"It's all good, don't worry about it," I say as I drop my hands immediately, my gaze falling over the absolute specimen in front of me.

His dark hair is wet, haphazardly falling in his amber eyes, which is bad enough, because the sight of a wet, surprised Geo Graves is attractive in ways I can't even *begin* to try and describe, but my gaze falls to his chest.

To the giant black cross that stretches across his well-defined pecs and six pack, and it keeps trailing lower until I see the cross disappear beneath his towel.

My towel, that is wrapped over his absolutely vicious fucking V.

Fuck.

Geo grabs his towel tightly, clutching his makeup bag across his chest.

"Sorry, just, uh... needed my face stuff." He looks at me, batting those dark eyelashes as he chews on his lower lip, his eyebrows furrowing.

A strange tension builds, and I suddenly feel very warm.

Geo clears his throat, his fingers gripping his bag tightly. "Got it," he squeaks.

I shake my head, heading for the doorway.

"Yeah, of course. I'll just, uh—you go that way, I'll go this way."

Once the door is closed behind me, I let out a slow breath, removing my boxers and heading straight for the shower.

Sliding under the hot water, I run my hands through my hair, trying to focus on the task at hand. My cock jumps with excitement, and I shake my head.

"No, absolutely not," I tell myself, lathering up my hair with shampoo.

I close my eyes, letting the hot water sluice over my skin. My cock throbs, needing attention, and I curse under my breath.

I can't. I fucking can't.

He's right across the hall, for fuck's sake!

What if he comes back in here for something?

Though that thought doesn't strike fear in my cock like it should. Not one fucking bit, and I slam my hand against the tile, shaking my head.

Do I want him to walk in here and find me

fucking my fist in the shower while I think about him?

I can't say I dislike that idea, and I know I should.

Geo might be okay with my being gay in theory, but knowing Geo's general disposition about sex in general, I'm not entirely sure he'd be okay with that.

I adjust my cock, turn off the shower, climb out, and grab my towel, wrapping it tightly around my waist.

"Show some fucking restraint," I say to the mirror as I run my hands through my hair.

I push myself away from the sink, opening the door. I catch Geo, sitting on the edge of the bed, staring at his phone, the light casting an almost angelic glow on his face. I try not to stare, but the sun shining through the window on his pale, defined back and shoulders makes him look younger. Softer.

Pretty.

He flashes his gaze up at me, but he doesn't say anything. His phone chirps, but he doesn't answer.

"You going to get that?" I ask as I shift my stance, my cock twitching behind my towel.

No! I said restraint, damn it!

"It can wait," he replies as he sets his phone down on the bed beside him, standing up.

I fight not to look down, because I know if I do, I'll see him in his fucking underwear and I'll never be able to erase *that* image. I'll see that badass cross dipping below his waistband, and I'll be too fucking tempted to touch him and see just where it ends.

I suck in a deep breath, and turn around, heading for my bedroom, and I shut the door.

I know I should feel victorious because I didn't look.

And I really fucking wanted to.

When I finish the last button on my shirt, I look at myself in the mirror, letting out a deep breath, and then I open the door.

CHAPTER 17

GEO

ZEB PARKS THE CAR, but neither of us move.

I stare at the house, noting it looks no different than the last time I saw it.

It's not ominous looking or anything, but it's pretty large and spacious because even before my mother started managing local artists, she and my dad used to entertain a lot.

"You okay?" Zeb asks, pulling my attention.

I turn to him. The dark plum of his shirt makes his tan complexion almost golden. His green eyes stand out against the dark hair framing his face, speckled along his jaw.

He was never unattractive as a teenager, but there's no denying he's had the fucking glow up of the century.

New demographics, indeed.

"It's just dinner, right?" My gaze flashes to his perfect, pink, full lips, thinking about Mateo and Dare's words.

You got this.

Zeb nods. "Don't worry, if things go south, I got your back," he says, offering me a small smile.

And for the moment, that's enough.

We climb out of the truck and Zeb comes around to my side with an encouraging smile on his lips.

Zeb sets his hand on the small of my back, giving me a nudge.

Katy all but crashes into us.

"Oh my God!" She squeals as she throws her arms around me. "Look at you!"

Zeb laughs, but he doesn't remove his hand.

When my mom and dad round the corner, I don't miss the look of happiness on their faces.

Zeb drops his hand, and immediately, I feel the emptiness, my skin still burning from the heat of his palm through my shirt.

"Welcome home, baby," my mother says as she pulls me into her arms.

Reflexively, I lift my arms to hold onto her as she kisses me on my cheek.

I flash my gaze at Zeb who offers me a reassuring smile, and I close my eyes and wrap my arms around my mom, and pray to make it through this dinner unscathed.

AFTER DINNER, a couple glasses of wine, and a healthy helping of my mother's apple pie, I am more than ready to crash.

Zeb opens the car door for me, and I relax instantly once the door is shut.

"Now, that wasn't so bad, was it?" he asks, casting me a sexy smile.

I look at him in the amber light of his truck, the way the shadows fall across his face.

God, he is gorgeous.

"Guess not," I reply as he turns the car on.

He nods to the radio dial. "You pick this time," he says softly.

I reach for the dial, fiddling until I find a station I like. I stop when I hear Kenya Grace's

Strangers, my thoughts falling back to his voice, the way he sang *"We'll get in your car and you'll lean to kiss me..."* so fucking *perfectly.*

I watch him as he drives, one sizable arm resting on his windowsill, while his other hand palms the steering wheel.

I can't take my damn eyes off of him.

Maybe it's the wine, maybe it's the fact today wasn't a total disaster, maybe it's just my mid-life fucking crisis obliterating me to pieces.

"Can I ask you an insanely personal question?" I ask softly, my heart in my throat.

Zeb turns to raise an eyebrow at me. "That depends on what it is," he says with a grin.

I lick my lips, unable to tear my gaze away from his absolutely beautiful profile, the way the muscles in his wrist and his forearms draw my attention in a way I know I've never noticed on anyone else.

"How did you know you were gay?"

Zeb pauses, and for a minute I think he's not going to answer me.

"It wasn't any one thing. More like, it was a bunch of little things," he says honestly.

"Like what?" I inquire as he turns down the

road I'm starting to recognize as the main drag to his house.

"Well, for starters, my crushes were never girls my age," he replies with a laugh. "That was probably a big one, but there were other things, too." He pulls his truck up to his driveway, but he doesn't shut it off.

"Like what?" I ask, shifting in my seat. The motion puts me closer to him since there isn't a console between us.

He chews his bottom lip, his green eyes sparkling the same way they did when I ran into him into the hallway earlier.

"I think a big one was when all I could think about was kissing this guy I was fucking crazy about," he says quietly, his gaze flashing to me. "It was brutal. Literally, all I could think about when I was around him."

A wave of heat overtakes me as the longing in his eyes registers.

"Did you do it?" I ask, my gaze fixated on his glittering eyes. "Kiss him, I mean?"

Zeb licks his lips, swallowing harshly, and he leans in closer to me.

Without thinking, I lean in, my gaze dipping to his mouth.

And then it hits me like a fucking brick.

I. Leaned. In.

Oh, fuck.

"Nope," he says, his breath warm on my skin. "Didn't think he wanted me to. Didn't think he was into me like that."

I set my hand on the seat in the space between us, noting how the edges of my fingers graze his knee as I do so. He shifts a little closer, the motion putting my entire hand on his knee.

I lean in an inch, feeling like I'm on the edge of a fucking cliff. My body heats as my heart beats faster, so fast I think it's going to explode out of my fucking chest.

I slide my hand just an inch over his knee, resting it. My palms heat, and I think I am *Hellbound* for sure.

"What if he did? Want you to, I mean?" I ask calmly. "If said he wanted you to... would you?"

Zeb's breath is steady, and he implores my gaze. "Fuck yes, I would," he breathes. "In a heartbeat."

I move closer until the edge of my knee brushes against his and my hand slides up his leg, resting on his thigh where I leave it.

He closes his eyes for a moment as he bites

his lip, opening them to implore my gaze once more. "Is that what you want, Geo?" he whispers. His verdant gaze falls to my lips. "For me to kiss you? Here? Now?"

I don't miss the way his voice shakes, and it's a strange sort of comfort knowing he's just as scared as I am.

"Yes," I whisper shakily, because I do, and the levity of that truth is not lost on me.

Zeb reaches out, settling his fingers on my throat, his gaze focused on mine for what feels like an eternity until he moves and he pulls me in, his lips grazing over mine.

My entire body responds to his mouth in a way I've never responded to anyone. It feels unlike anything else I've ever felt.

Every muscle in my body loosens, my limbs suddenly like jello, and I feel like I might actually pass out.

I grab onto his neck, grounding myself to him as I process the smooth, soft feel of his lips on mine. The way they move slowly, almost angelically. His sweet tonka-bean teakwood scent surrounds me with familiarity and comfort.

A soft groan escapes my throat, and I don't even try to fucking hide it. I can't.

He breaks away slowly, his breath heavy as the sound of sexy "uh huh's" echo in the space.

It's like I've finally awakened from a spell I didn't even know I was under.

I tighten my grip on his neck, his skin warm against my palm, and I crush my lips against his once more.

CHAPTER 18

ZEB

I'M worried any minute I'm going to wake up in my bed and realize this is all a dream.

An absolutely perfect dream, one I thought I'd never actually touch.

Geo's right hand slides up my thigh, squeezing faintly, while his left hand grips my throat. His lips aren't soft by any means, or shaky, not like I'd expect.

They are brutal.

Harsh, hurried, hungry.

Geo kisses me like he's fucking starving and I'm a bowl full of maraschino cherries. His tongue slides into my mouth without resistance, grazing the edge of my own, and then he just stops.

Gone is the rush, and its place is a softer, sweeter kiss, a touch of grace to even out the rush as he swiftly pulls away.

Fuck restraint.

Fuck it all to hell.

He looks up at me, biting his kiss-swollen bottom lip, dark eyes full of fire.

"I'm going to, uh... we should probably head into the house," he says, his voice a little darker, raspier than usual.

"Yeah, of course. Right," I say, shaking my head as I turn the car off and try to get my bearings about me. "It's late, I'm sure you're beat." I open the door, my heart beating in my chest like a damn freight train.

What just happened here?

I fumble with my keys as we walk to the door.

Should I say something?

I should say *something,* right?

I steal a glance at him underneath my porch lights, dark hair a little messy, his pupils a little blown, and his lips still perfectly swollen from our *kiss.*

I kissed him, and he fucking kissed me *back.*

A myriad of emotions swirl inside of me as I open the door to let us in.

I have a hundred questions I want to ask him. I know sexuality is a pretty fluid scale, but Geo's never shown *any* inclination of interest in the same sex. Or the opposite sex, if we're being totally honest, here. I mean, I *know* he's had girlfriends, but he never seemed particularly interested in the way most guys are when they have a girlfriend.

I close the door and lock it, and he saunters across my living room, his pale, defined forearms standing out against his rolled up pale blue button down sleeves.

He turns to me, flashing his dark gaze at me, and I think if the devil were real, he'd look exactly like Geo Graves at this precise moment.

Older.

Hotter.

Dark hair all messed up, fiery gaze and kiss-swollen lips, hands in his pockets.

I am so fucking *Hellbound.*

"Good night," he says, and with that, he leaves me in my living room.

I touch my mouth, noting I can still taste him on my tongue, and my cock is still hard as a fucking rock.

I know I need to be careful.

I know that one kiss doesn't mean Geo is all in. Everyone gets curious, sometimes.

Right?

That's all it was, just a kiss. Maybe a wine-induced curiosity.

Except, something tells me that's not entirely the case.

I run my hands over my face as I fall into my couch, feeling overwhelmed.

He asked me how I *knew* I was gay, which he's right, is an extremely personal question.

But maybe there was an actual reason he asked me.

Maybe, just maybe, Geo isn't as straight we all thought he was, and he's just now realizing it at thirty-nine.

I stare off down the hall, at his shut door.

Memories flood me of all the moments I took for granted. The boys I messed around with as a teenager when we were "experimenting" or just fucking around.

I was into whatever I could get from those guys, because I enjoyed the rush of it. The secrecy of it. Making them come in the locker room before practice, getting them all hot and bothered in the library during study sessions.

Getting fucked in the bathroom at the parties we weren't supposed to be at.

But it was also confusing as hell because I knew I wanted more, but I didn't think more was an option at the time.

I'm not sure it's an option now, either, but I want it all the same.

I want it now more than I think I ever did, but I also know how dangerous it is to want Geo Graves.

He broke my heart before.

Will he do it again?

It's still dark out when I wake up, but I've always been a bit of an early riser, even despite the fact I work late a lot when I'm out on gigs.

But there's something relaxing and easy about being up before everyone else is.

I squint into the darkness, noting the clock reads five fifteen. I shut my alarm off before it can go off and wake Geo, since he's right across the hall.

I quietly crack open my door, noting his door isn't completely shut. I move to shut it, stopping as I peer into the darkness. The sliver of light from the hall seeps into the room, casting an almost godly glow directly on his dark form. He rolls over, groaning in his sleep, and I quietly shut the door, my stolen moment gone too far.

I know it's probably rare he gets this sort of time in general, so the last thing I want to do is interrupt the guy's long overdue chance to sleep in.

I slip away, grabbing a towel from my hallway closet, and make my way to the bathroom. The heat of the shower is welcome and I can't help but let out a groan of my own from the warmth.

I work up a lather over my chest, which is always somewhat of a feat because the suds always multiply between my coarse hair and it takes forever to rinse, but I don't mind the extra time, or the hair in general.

It beats having to shave and trim my entire chest and torso every two days, too.

I run my hands over my chest, down my stomach, until I settle at my semi-erect cock.

I know it's early, and he's passed the fuck out, so I don't feel as guilty about taking care of myself because there isn't any real threat of being discovered.

I close my eyes, tipping my head back as I let the water run down my skin, lazily stroking my cock. I let my mind wander to the previous night, to that *kiss.*

Fuck, I can't remember the last time I *kissed* a guy and got so worked up.

But Geo isn't just *any guy.*

His hand on my thigh, so dangerously close to my fucking erection, was more of a turn on than I want to admit.

A part of me wanted to shift so I could feel his hand on my aching cock, while the sensible part of me was terrified he'd find my fucking swollen cock and freak the fuck out.

It's one thing to kiss a guy, but it's another thing completely to touch his solid dick, *knowing* full well *you* are the reason for it.

My thoughts travel down that fantastical

road, thinking about Geo touching *my* dick. Stroking it with his perfect, masculine fingers through my pants while driving that wicked tongue into my mouth.

"Fucking hell," I curse under my breath as I come. I pump out the remaining bits of my cum, letting out a sigh of relief as I clean myself up.

I step out of the shower, drying off quickly, catching my reflection in the mirror. With my towel wrapped around my waist, I push open the door, head for my bedroom, glancing at Geo's door.

It's popped back open again, and I stop for a moment, panic flooding me.

I push the door open slightly, if only to settle my anxiety. Sure enough, Geo's still sprawled out on the bed, in the same lifeless position as he was before.

"Get a hold of yourself, Zeb," I mumble as I turn for my bedroom.

I change into a pair of comfortable sweatpants, grab my phone and earbuds, and head for the kitchen to set about my morning the same way I always do.

Lady Gaga serenades my ears as I open my

fridge, grabbing fresh eggs, cheese, vegetables, and, of course, bacon.

I settle into the motions, humming and singing along while I crack and whisk my eggs.

I can't resist moving to the beat, because honestly, who can?

Lady Gaga is a fucking legend.

I sing about monstrous men eating my fucking heart as I fire up the stove. The flame rises as I croon out the lyrics, getting into the crunchy beats. The eggs sizzle in the pan and I watch as the golden liquid spreads throughout the pan. I rotate the pan by moving my wrist, watching as it covers all the open spots.

The smell of coffee permeates the air and I work on flipping my omelet as the drop comes. I flip it and catch it with ease, spinning around to grab my mug of coffee, and I stop dead in my tracks.

Geo leans against my refrigerator, those delicious arms crossed in front of his bare, tattooed chest. His dark hair sticks out in disarray, but it isn't a bad look on him. Coupled with his gray sweatpants, and his thick, tortoise shell *glasses*, he looks...

Perfect.

Fucking perfect.

I take my earbuds out, immediately tensing.

"Did I wake you up? Fuck, I'm sorry. I—"

He shrugs, letting out a chuckle. "Oh no, don't let me stop you. Please, continue."

I move for the pan, realizing if I don't grab my omelet, it's going to fucking burn.

Shit!

"I, uh—" I clear my throat as I turn off the fire, plating up my omelet. "Guess I got carried away," I say as I card a hand through my hair.

Geo's gaze flashes to the earbuds in my hand.

"Didn't peg you for a Gaga fan," he says with a grin. He pushes off of my fridge, taking slow strides toward me.

I set my earbuds down on the island and glance at his waist, noting the way his sweatpants hang off of his form. I'm trying *not* to notice the prolific outline of his swinging cock or where the edges of his tattoo disappear.

It's like a fucking neon sign, I swear.

"Didn't anyone tell you? When you get your gay card you have to choose a Gaga song. Like a Pokémon."

Geo's eyes widen, his eyebrows furrowing. "Seriously?"

His innocence and naivety should not be as cute as it is, but it's fucking adorable.

"No," I tease him as I pour him a cup of coffee.

He smirks, letting out a laugh. "Judas," he says with a grin. "My favorite Gaga song. The video was *sick*."

Then he shrugs, singing out those undeniable lyrics about being a holy fool, while rolling his eyes.

I take a slow step forward, singing out the next line, raising an eyebrow at him as I smirk about being in love with Judas anyway.

And like the devil he is, he grins, looking at me over his glasses.

"Fucking genius."

I take a sip of my coffee and he wrinkles his nose.

"What?"

"How can you drink that shit black?"

I shrug. "There's half and half in the fridge if you want it."

He opens the fridge and I don't miss the way the light illuminates him.

I watch as he pours the liquid into his cup, my gaze transfixed on how unbelievably hot this man is at quarter to six in the morning. It's fucking criminal. I never wake up looking this good rolling out of bed.

"Was that your idea or the label's?" I ask, nodding at his tattoo as he stirs his coffee.

"Oh, this?" He points to his chest with one hand. "Label suggested I should get some ink, and I just figured if I was going to do it, I only wanted to do it once, so... I picked the biggest thing I could think of."

"Really?" I ask, leaning against the island.

Geo shifts his weight. "Really. It was going to be this or angel wings on my back, but I figured people would see my chest more than my back, so..." He looks away for a moment, almost as if he's embarrassed.

"What about you?" he asks, taking a pull of his coffee.

"What about me?" I grab my omelet, setting the plate between us, and grab two forks. I pass him one and he takes it.

"You have any tattoos I don't know about?"

I smirk at him as I dive into my omelet. "One."

Geo raises his eyebrows. "Really? Where? What is it?"

"It's a secret."

Geo rolls his eyes, huffing in annoyance. "What did you get it on your ass or something?"

I smirk at him and don't miss the way his cheeks stain with scarlet blush.

"You got a fucking tattoo on your *ass?*"

I laugh with a shrug. "I was twenty-one!"

He shakes his head, laughing, and the sound is so pure and genuine, I can't help but smile.

I rarely think about the *Hellbound* devil tail tattoo I got on my ass on a dare, because I can't see it. I forget it's there half the time. Until someone points it out, of course, after they take my fucking pants off, which is always an awkward conversation.

I reach out without thinking, setting my hand on his hip, tracing my thumb over the black outline of his cross just above his waistband.

His skin is smooth and hard against digit, and I marvel at the intricate outline, the inside filled in black ink. It really is a stunning tattoo, even if it takes up the majority of his chest and torso.

"How long did that take?" I ask.

I trace my fingers up the outline, following the trail across his chest. I half expect him to push me away, because I know it's kind of an inappropriate touch, but he doesn't push me away and that spark threatens to catch again.

"Eight sessions, about six hours each."

I whistle. "Must've hurt like a bitch." I graze my fingers over the ink that just grazes the edge of his nipples.

"Wasn't that bad," he says, shifting his weight. He settles his hand on my hip, and I feel his heartbeat beneath my fingertips, where I stop my hand over his right pec, brushing my thumb and forefinger over the defined muscle there.

Racing.

I drop my hand, but he doesn't remove his from where he touches me. He tugs just the slightest, and I let him pull me closer.

The light of the morning threatens to break through the last moments of darkness, the haze of dawn.

"What are you doing, Geo?" I ask, licking my lips.

"I don't' know," he says honestly. "I just..."

His gaze searches mine, his amber eyes glistening with flecks of gold in the morning light.

"I spent a lot of years being told the things I

felt weren't right," he says softly. "Kinda fucked me up, and not in a good way."

His fingers squeeze my hip carefully, his palm warm against my skin.

"I don't want to second-guess what feels right, you know?" he says. He looks up at me, and my heart wants to break.

Without thinking, I reach out, settling my hand against his neck as I capture his gaze.

Geo doesn't move. He only looks up at me with a tenderness that is as vulnerable as it is hopeful, and my own heart wants to leap out of my fucking chest.

"And this feels... right?" I brush my fingers softly against the edges of his hair and he responds by pulling me against him.

"Yes," he says, closing his eyes as he nuzzles his cheek into my palm. The motion makes me want to melt like the butter in the fucking skillet.

He lets out a heavy breath. "I like how it feels." He swallows harshly. Flashing those dark eyes up at me, he breathes, "I like how it feels when you look at me like that."

I brush my thumb over his lips from the sudden movement, and the smoothness beneath my fingertip threatens to bring back the memory of exactly what those lips feel like against my own.

And almost as if he just *knows*, he responds to my touch.

"I like how it feels when you touch me. When you *kiss* me."

"Is that right?" I ask, softly hooking my thumb under his chin. I look him in his eyes, knowing I'm signing my fucking death certificate.

He nods. "I feel like I've been dying a slow death for years, but now I'm *alive.*"

His words are pure and honest. Brutal, in a different kind of way.

He grabs me by the neck, pulling me toward him, and I don't fight him. Not one fucking bit, because it does feel right.

Everything about him feels so undeniably right.

Geo kisses me slowly, his fingers sliding into my hair, and he grips the locks tight.

I stumble a bit as he moves backward, shifting our weight until he is beneath me. I brace my hands on both sides of him, boxing him in.

His fingers travel over my jaw, hands

traipsing down my chest slowly, delicately. He moves his touch across my hips, twisting his fingers in the hair above my navel, grazing over the waistband of my jeans gracefully, carefully, but with reverence.

Geo Graves explores me like an uncharted map, his touch making my entire body heat like a flame.

He rises just the slightest from his momentary cage, arching his back as he opens his mouth, one hand finding my neck again as he squeezes lightly.

His tongue finds mine quickly and his kiss turns hungry, heated, and rough, grace giving way to the rush once more, and I settle my hand on his hip, and then I feel it.

The heaviness of his fucking cock, hard against my own.

I groan as I instinctively grind against him.

His body is solid against mine as he ravages my mouth. His tongue caresses mine fervently, and he moans as his hand on my neck slides up into my hair, once more grabbing a fistful of it in his hand.

A deep groan escapes his throat as he *thrusts* himself against me.

It's a startling contrast to how he normally is; shy, sweet, innocent.

But I can't deny I like him like this.

Hard, needy, and beneath me.

"Geo..." I breathe his name as I try to find my way back to the present. Because the way he's touching me, kissing me, is like an out of body experience.

His breath catches and I worry maybe I've gone too far, but before I can break away, he moans into my mouth and his entire body tenses.

"Fuck, Zeb." His voice is strained, and he grabs onto me for dear life with one hand, the other finding its resting place right over my cock. He doesn't grab me or squeeze me, but I don't miss the heat of his touch or the way his fingers tremble against me.

I grind myself against his palm, and his fingers move of their own accord, rubbing over my shaft and head.

"Zeb, I'm going to—" He closes his eyes, breathing deep. "Fuck!" he cries as my phone rings loudly, practically jumping off the counter.

I'd recognize the ringtone anywhere.

It's Katy.

Geo lets out a guilty groan as buries his head

in my shoulder, and I don't miss how his cock throbs against mine through his sweatpants as his shoulders tense against me.

His lips against my skin are like fire as he lets out a shaky, hurried breath.

Instinctively, I wrap my arm around him, pulling him close as he pants against my chest.

"It's okay, you're okay," I say, because I can barely breathe myself, and I'm not all that sure I am indeed, okay.

Geo's breath against my skin is hot and all consuming and I struggle to find my own center at the moment.

Fucking hell...

His phone rings from its spot next to the coffee pot.

Katy's ringtone echoes in symphony with Geo's phone.

"Fuck," I curse as I move away, even though I don't want to. But I know if I don't answer, she'll just keep calling.

Geo braces his arms out against the counter, his breaths still heavy and labored. He looks up at me, his pupils still blown, lips still kiss-swollen.

I punch the green icon on my phone.

"What?" I snap at her, probably more harshly than I should. Katy doesn't notice, though.

"Sorry to wake you, but, like, this is super important," she drawls.

I glance at Geo, who's catching his breath, focused on answering his own phone.

"It better be," I gripe.

"So, mom just got a call from the coordinator at the Gardens," she chirps excitedly. "And they had a cancellation last minute, and they asked her if she knew anyone, and—-"

My blood chills. I purposefully took this week off to be *home*, to spend time with my friend.

"Anyway, I told them we'd take it."

"Katy..." I pinch the bridge of my nose. "I can't play a set today..."

"It's an hour set, Zeb, it won't kill us. You'll be in and out."

Geo watches me intently.

"I don't even have a set list prepared." I huff in annoyance.

"Do it," Geo says, making me turn around.

"What?"

"Is my brother up already?" she asks.

"I can't. I—"

"Yes, you can. You can and you will," he says sternly.

"I wasn't planning on playing anywhere while you were here." I shake my head, feeling more on the spot now than when Geo was fucking kissing me.

"Oh, you should totally bring him, Zeb! It'll be just like old times."

Geo crosses his arms, takes two steps toward me, and plucks the phone out of my hands.

And I do nothing to stop him.

"What time?" he asks, and I can hear Katy chattering. "Okay, text me the set list." Ne nods, smirking at me. "Yeah, that sounds good. We'll be there," he says, hangs up, and tosses the phone at me.

I barely catch it.

"You go on at noon," he says, and drains the last of his coffee.

CHAPTER 19

Geo

There is no question about it, I'm one hundred percent gay for Zebulon Ingram.

I might have been able to write off our kiss in his truck as research, maybe I could have even attributed it to just being in the heat of the moment because I was trying to process, well, everything going on in my head.

But there was no writing off the way I felt when I saw him through the sliver of the open door this morning, naked in his shower.

There was no ignoring how my heart raced

when he ran his fingers over my skin, tracing the lines of my tattoo.

There was no denying how hard I was, knowing he was hard, too.

Because of me.

Because he *liked* me.

He liked touching me, kissing me, holding me.

Grinding his cock against me.

And even if I could explain those things away, there was no explaining away the mess I made in my fucking sweatpants because I was so fucking aroused by all of it.

By him.

Familiar feelings of guilt and shame threatened to resurface, combating with the pleasure that lit me up like a star, trying to sink its poison into me and ruin what felt so fucking *right*.

So, I did the only thing I could think of and reached for my salvation.

I reached for Zeb.

And he didn't push me away. He let me bury my face in his shoulder, and he told me it was *okay*.

He didn't judge me, didn't look at me like I was broken. He just held me and said it was okay, and that moment felt so right. *He* felt more right than anyone else ever has.

I watch him, one hand gripping his steering wheel, with the other dangling over the door with his arm partway outside his window.

"What?" he asks. "Do I have something on my face?"

The hot air filtering in through the open windows does nothing to help quell the heat that forms in my cheeks.

"Nope, just appreciating the view."

I don't miss the way his eyes crinkle a bit when he smiles.

"You keep saying swoony things like that, sunshine, and I'm going to have to turn this fucking truck around." His tone isn't angry or sarcastic. It's humorous.

"And stand up my sister? Please. You and I both know she'd hunt you down and you'd never hear the end of it."

He laughs, shaking his head as my phone chirps with a text.

It's Mateo. *Kevin get ahold of you?*

I haven't heard from Kevin since we got in, and I told him I was going to be unavailable until Wednesday, when Zeb agreed to drop me back off at the hotel for sound check at the stadium.

No, what's up?

Mateo texts back quickly. *Concert Friday is canceled. Rescheduled for Saturday.*

Shit.

I'd planned on being back at the hotel and staying overnight for the concert Thursday into Friday. Saturday is my birthday.

"Mateo?" Zeb's voice is clipped.

"Yeah. He said the concert's postponed until Saturday."

"So… what does that mean for you?"

I shift in my seat. "Well, it means I've got a couple extra days of R&R for one, but it also means that I'll be leaving right after the show, Monday morning."

"Oh," he says as my phone chirps again.

Dare wants to know if you did the lean. I told him it's none of his business, but he's insisting *I ask you how your* research *is going.*

I shake my head, a smile forming on my lips. I don't know how I got this lucky in life, to have such good friends in a business where so many people are cutthroat, but I thank God all the same.

Yes. But if we're being technical, he leaned first.

I flush, biting my lip as I steal a glance at Zeb's profile, my gaze settling on his perfect mouth, on his dark facial hair, remembering the scratchy feel against my skin as he kissed me this morning.

My phone chirps like a hungry baby bird as a slew of texts come in, and I know Dare has abducted Mateo's phone from all the emojiis and the OMGGGG's, and a *Yasss G! Get that D!*

When we park, Zeb gives me a sideways glance.

"What?"

"We didn't have to do this, you know," he says, flashing me with a smirk.

"I know." I shrug. "But I want to see you play. For real."

"I could play for you at home." He sighs.

"No, no. I want to see you in all your glory."

"Mhmmm." He opens the door, and I follow suit, helping him to unload his equipment. The sun shines down on me, hot and unforgiving.

The parking lot is already starting to get full, and I'm thankful for the moment that I decided not to don my normal *Gravedigger* costume.

I'd showered, laid out my black mesh tank, and jeans. I even had all my hair and face stuff set up, but then I took one look in Zeb's bathroom mirror, at myself in my glasses and sweatpants, and I just wanted to be *me* for a day.

So, I grabbed one of my white tees I usually use for layering, and instead of jeans, I went for a pair of black athletic shorts that I would usually reserve for the gym, grabbed my incognito baseball cap, and didn't put my contacts in.

I felt like a million bucks.

Though, I'm sure kissing Zeb might have contributed to the feeling, too.

Good God, no one has ever kissed me like *that*.

"You owe me later, you know." Zeb's voice pulls my attention.

I turn to see him leaning against his truck with a dark look in his eye that makes my stomach flip.

Yep, I think I most definitely identify as a Zebsexual.

If I'm gay, I'm gay for *him*.

Because as far as I'm concerned, no one is as perfect as this man.

"Oh, do I now?" I cross my arms, entering

his space. He reaches out in the slightest, setting his hand on my hip. He tugs me softly and I shift closer to him, imploring him with my gaze.

"Yup." His green eyes glitter with flirtation as he leans in closer to my space, capturing my gaze, his lips inches away from mine.

I'm acutely aware that we are in public and anyone can see us. Including my sister, who is supposed to be meeting us here. Panic starts to build as those familiar feelings of guilt threaten to upend me, but I take one look at Zeb and they seem to get a little quieter.

I lean into him, into his space, flashing my gaze up at him.

"I'll buy you a sour apple martini later." I smirk.

"I'll hold you to that, sunshine," he drawls, and I don't think twice about kissing him.

I break away, noting his grin as we pick up his equipment and head inside.

Katy arrives not long after, but she isn't alone.

Katy hooks her arm in Zeb's. "The talent and I must be off now. Autographs are fifteen dollars and our booth is over there," she teases, winking at me.

Zeb rolls his eyes. "This is your fault," he says, narrowing his eyes at me. "Remember that."

My mother laughs. "Break a leg, Zebulon!"

He smiles as Katy pulls him in the other direction, leaving my mother and I alone.

Fuck.

"So... cancellation, huh?" I ask, not knowing what else to say.

She shrugs, hooking her arm in mine as we head for the seats that are starting to fill in.

"God works in mysterious ways," she says, and I purse my lips.

"Yeah, I guess he does."

We take our seats, sitting three rows back from the stage.

"I heard your concert was canceled."

I cross my legs. "Postponed, not canceled," I say.

She waves at me dismissively. "That means you have a little more time off, right? More time to spend with us? With Zeb?"

I look at her, feeling on the spot. Her words don't feel suspicious, but my mother isn't one of those outwardly deceptive people.

She's like one of those little African cats that

look like kittens, but are one of the most vicious predators alive.

"And my friends," I say defensively.

Mateo *did* say we should hang out. Maybe I should take him up on it, bring Zeb.

Maybe it would be fun to hang out with another couple?

I blink as the thought lands.

Are we... we aren't a couple, are we?

I'm not entirely sure *what* we are, to be honest, because this really is a new demographic for me, and I don't have the best track record with my previous demographic, either.

Do I *want* us to be a couple?

What would that even look like?

Me in LA with Kevin and my label breathing down my neck while he's here playing shows with my sister?

I don't have time to process my thoughts as the lights dim, and Zeb comes out on stage. I look around at the cozy atmosphere. There's a bar in the corner with someone pouring champagne, and I vow to stay as far away from that as possible.

Apparently, I have no filter when I drink champagne.

Zeb takes the stage, slinging his acoustic over his shoulder. The lights make his dark hair shimmer with copper highlights.

He introduces himself, his expression full of light and excitement. He strums out a few chords I recognize instantly. Whitney Houston's *I Want To Dance With Somebody.*

"Oh, I love it when he performs this," my mom says, nudging my arm.

I look at her as his voice fills the air. "You've seen him? More than once?" I ask, dumbfounded.

"He's quite popular," she says with a grin. "With the girls and the boys."

I feel frozen by her words.

Does she know?

I blink as I turn to focus on him.

My mom links her arm in mine, running her nails along my forearm.

He croons out Whitney's words, and I can't deny they sound good in the timbre of his deep, sexy voice.

He rolls his words, breathy and emotional as the guitar plays.

Zeb croons on about wanting to feel the heat

with somebody, closing his eyes, and I feel my mother's nails squeezing my arm.

"He's so good," she sighs. "Too bad he's not in it for the fame like you are. Because, can you *imagine*?"

Her praise isn't lost on me, and I can't argue with her.

I've always known he was talented, that he had that "thing."

The confidence, the sex appeal, the voice.

Not a day goes by where I don't wonder what things would be like if he came with me to Hollywood.

Would we have just been the best of friends, writing music and selling out shows?

Would we be like we are now?

Zeb opens his eyes, staring right at me as he sings about needing a man to take a chance, and I wonder as he smirks at me, if I can be that man.

I watch in awe through every song, but the last one is the best.

Beautiful Things by Benson Boone.

By the end of the show, he's traded his acoustic for an electric guitar, and his black button up is rolled up to his elbows.

He cries out, his voice the most beautiful thing I think I've ever heard.

He closes his eyes, and the emotion in his voice, his presence, is undeniable as he sings about not wanting to lose the beautiful things he's got.

When the song ends, the crowd applauds.

My mother wipes her thumb underneath my eye.

I shake her off. "What the hell, mom?"

She smiles at me, a sparkle in her blue eyes. "Got a little something there," she says. "Must be your allergies, baby."

Allergies, my fucking ass.

We both stand, and she links her arm in mine once more.

"Told you he was good." She leads me through the gardens, and for a moment I think maybe she has changed. But then she speaks. "So... how are things in Hollywood, baby?"

I tense. Like a shark, my mother can smell fear, so I try to remain indifferent.

"Good, I guess."

She casts me a rueful gaze. "Your last two albums barely scratched the billboard charts," she says pensively.

I frown. Great, she's been keeping tabs. Though, I don't know why she wouldn't, if only for a moment precisely like this one. To throw it in my face and make me feel like a failure.

"It's not the songs that are the issue," I bite.

She sighs. "So what is it then?" she asks as we stop at an arrangement of cactuses.

"Does it really matter?" I ask, pulling my arm away from her.

"Of course it matters. If it's something I can help you with—"

I shake my head. "Doubt it, mom."

She sighs, looking up at the flower arch in front of us. "Are you seeing anyone?" she asks, and I close my eyes.

I want to say yes, but I don't even know if I am technically *seeing* anyone. I'm kissing him. I'm coming in my fucking pants, but I don't know if I'm messing around, seeing, or dating him.

So, I settle on the safe answer, which is probably truer than I want to admit.

"No," I reply.

She purses her lips. "You're going to be forty Saturday, baby."

I grind my teeth. "Yeah, thanks for the reminder, I totally forgot." I roll my eyes.

"I'm just saying, you aren't getting any younger. You can't be a bachelor forever."

The audacity of this woman.

How dare she tell me I need to settle down, I need to find someone, when she and my father were so adamant I remain *abstinent* for the majority of my fucking life.

It's because of *them*, because of their "morals" that I am the way I am.

"You think I *want* to be alone, mom?" I snap, feeling a flush of heat.

"Of course not," she says, her eyebrows furrowing. "I didn't mean—"

"No, you never do, that's the problem mom. You never *mean* to hurt me, but you do."

"What is that's supposed to mean?" she asks.

"Nothing." I hold myself tight.

"Baby, talk to me, tell me what's wrong..."

I shake my head, and that's when I see them. Katy and Zeb.

"I can't do this with you, mom, I just can't."

Zeb catches my gaze, and I focus on walking toward him. One step, two step, three.

Katy looks up at me, her eyebrows furrowed. "Geo, what—"

"Take me home, please," I say, feeling the cyclone of guilt and shame starting to build. I have to focus on my breathing, focus on my nails digging into my skin.

Zeb's expression falls, and he reaches out for my arm. Katy's gaze falls to the spot where he touches me, but I don't have the guts to shake him off. His touch is warm, soothing, and I want nothing more than to fall into him.

"What happened?" she asks calmly.

"Mom happened," I reply as I bite my lip.

Katy sighs. "I'll talk to her."

"Come on." Zeb tugs my elbow.

Katy takes two steps, then turns around, staring at the both of us, then she shifts her gaze to Zeb. "Be careful, Z," she says, then turns around and heads toward our mother.

"What was that about?" I ask.

He slides his hand around my waist, settling his palm at the small of my back. "Nothing," he says, his voice faraway.

When we get to the car, I let go. I take my hat off, running my hands through my hair as he turns the car on. The tears come faster than they ever have before.

"She doesn't fucking get it," I say, shaking my head. "I spent twenty-nine years of my life being perfect. Poised, pure, and perfect. I sold records without ever having to show my fucking skin, but I was never allowed to be a fucking person!" I growl.

Zeb drives, sliding his hand over my knee, using the other to palm the steering wheel. "I know," he replies softly.

"My last two albums flopped miserably. Not because they weren't any good, because they were, but because—" I look out the window, the truth lodged in my throat. "I'm not sexy enough," I say, shaking my head.

"Are you fucking crazy?" Zeb says, surprise evident in his tone.

I turn to him, imploring him with my quickly blurring gaze. "Kinda hard to be sexy when you're a fucking forty-year-old virgin." I scoff. "Who's going to buy my sexy ass songs about fucking when I haven't fucked anyone?" I bite the words with venom, sinking into my seat. "God, you must think I'm an idiot," I say harshly.

Zeb's voice is smooth, comforting. "I don't think that at all, Geo."

I let out a frustrated sigh, looking to the bright blue sky.

God, give me strength to make it through this fucking week.

"Sorry, I shouldn't be unloading my defective sex shit and my mommy issues on you." I breathe deep. "Or my dying career shit." I rub my eyes. "I'm a fucking mess."

"No, Geo. You're not." His voice is soft, even. Warm and safe. "You are not defective," he says, squeezing my knee.

"I didn't even start masturbating until I was thirty, Zeb. And half the time, I couldn't even come because of all the fucking guilt. So, trust me, I am defective."

He's quiet for a moment as we pull up to his house, and then he shuts the car off. Neither of us move.

"Look at me," he says.

I run my hands over my face.

"Look at me, Geo."

I remove my hands, looking at his bright eyes. It's like seeing the sun.

He reaches out, pulling me closer into his space, and I move without question.

Into him, into his warm aura. His tonka bean-teakwood scent fills my lungs, and I feel like I'm on the edge of a cliff.

"You are *so fucking sexy.*" He reaches for my glasses, smirking. "And you're so fucking talented, and strong. Shit, you left to chase your dreams, man. And you made it a reality."

I don't fight the tear that rolls down my face, because the sincerity in his words are like a praise I never knew I needed.

And the way he looks at me, touches me... it's a forgiveness I don't deserve, but it's also something I desperately want.

His forgiveness, anyway.

"You are not defective. You are perfect. Just the way you fucking are."

There is a pregnant pause, and then he looks at me with the softest smile.

"You always were. Perfect, I mean. At least to me." His voice drops an octave as his gaze drops to my lips, then back up at me.

"Really?" I ask.

"Yeah. Really," he breathes.

Zeb brushes away that one kamikaze tear, and then he kisses me.

But this kiss... it's different from the others.

It's softer, deeper.

Zeb opens his mouth just the slightest, his tongue sliding into my mouth.

His lips are smooth, but his rough facial hair against my skin tickles.

And all at once, I know.

This... this is what I've been *waiting* for.

He's who I've been waiting for.

He breaks away, leaning his forehead against mine.

I sniffle as I grab his neck, squeezing lightly, savoring the sweetness of his kiss.

I never want to stop.

Ever.

Because when Zeb kisses me, it chases away all my demons.

It makes everything feel *right* again.

"Thank you," I whisper.

Zeb rustles the edges of my hair at the nape of my neck with his fingers, making my eyes flutter, making my heartbeat skip.

How can a simple touch do so much?

"Anytime, sunshine," he says, the corners of

his lips lifting up into a soft smile that melts my heart and makes my stomach do a little flip.

My mother was right.

He is good.

He's fucking perfect.

And I think I might be falling in love with him.

CHAPTER 20

I TOSS my keys on the counter as Geo brings in the last of my equipment.

I can't stop thinking about his words this morning, our damn near breathless makeout, coupled with his meltdown in my car.

Just this morning, he'd touched me, kissed me and told me he'd lived most of his life being told what he felt was *wrong,* or that he shouldn't feel it.

And because of everything he'd been through, he felt immense *guilt* over his feelings, and as such, exploring those feelings came at a cost for him.

But as I watch him plop down on my couch, grabbing for my acoustic, I can't help but see the strength in him he doesn't see in himself.

It takes a brave person to put their feelings first. To choose differently.

I can't help but think about my own defectiveness, and at that moment, I feel like I need to tell him the truth.

I take a seat next to him as he strums absent-mindedly.

"I'm defective, too, you know," I say casually.

Geo looks at me from beneath his thick glasses. "Somehow, I doubt that. But I appreciate you trying to make me feel better."

I shake my head. "I lost my virginity when I was fifteen."

His expression pales.

"I was dealing with my feelings the only way I knew how. Getting drunk and doing shit I wasn't supposed to."

"Is that something you regret?" he asks.

I shrug. "Not the initial moment. I learned pretty quickly what guys liked, and I thought if I could just do that... if I could just be good *enough,* that maybe one of them would actually want *me.*"

I shake my head. "But they didn't. Some came back, but, they didn't want anything other than sex, and I remember thinking, 'at least I'm good at that'." I scoff.

"And despite the fact I take care of myself, have a pretty good music career, and I'm clean as a damn whistle, I can't even keep a guy around for breakfast anymore. So, believe me when I tell you, you're not alone. We're all fucked up in our way, you know?"

Geo shifts closer to me as he strums away.

"What... what's it like?" he asks quietly.

I lean back on the couch, settling into the cushions. "What's what like?" I ask.

Geo licks his lips. "Sex. With... a guy, I mean. Does it hurt?" His dark eyes glisten, and I don't miss the way his fingers deftly strum away at the chords.

"Depends if you're the top or the bottom." I smirk.

Geo looks at me from beneath his thick frames, his lashes standing out against his pale skin.

"So… which are you?" he asks quietly, and I can't help my grin.

"Bottom."

Geo's cheeks flush. "Oh."

"And to answer your question, no. I mean, it hurts a little bit, but it's not a *bad* hurt. Unless I'm not prepped enough, of course, but…" I shrug. "Can I ask *you* a very personal question?" I say.

Geo nods. "Depends on what it is," he says carefully.

"Did you ever want to? Have sex, I mean. With any of your girlfriends?"

He stops playing, twisting his lips, and for a moment I think he's not going to answer me, but then he does.

"Not really. I was kinda burned on the whole fucking around thing after Tiffany."

I raise my eyebrow. I remember Geo dating a girl when I first met Katy. She was around for a couple dinners, but then she disappeared.

"What happened with Tiffany?" I ask.

"She was really, really pushy. She made me feel like I *needed* to give her *something*. She told me she needed to "connect" with me physically so we could be a better couple. So, I let her talk me into sucking my dick, and it was kind of the worst experience ever."

I raise my eyebrow. "Seriously?"

Geo nods. "Told you, defective."

He sets the guitar down on the ground. Then he shifts his position on the couch, putting us closer together. He catches my gaze.

"Sounds like she just wasn't very good at it." I smirk.

"Yeah, and on top of the teeth and the attitude, I couldn't... you know, and she kinda took it personally and broke up with me after that."

"Ouch." I rest my hand on his leg.

He shifts, leaning against the back of the couch. "I pretty much just kind of put a lock on it after that. I didn't want to deal with the guilt or the shame that came with that more than once."

"It didn't feel right," I say, squeezing his thigh.

Geo casts me a soft smirk. "No, it didn't." He slides his hand over my hip, and I let him pull me in. His dark gaze searches mine.

"Just for the record, I don't think you're

defective," he says. "I think those assholes just didn't deserve you."

"Probably not, but I didn't think I deserved them, either," I admit.

"You deserve so much more," he says, and the weight of his words are heavy in the air as I settle between his legs.

The motion makes the cushions dip from our combined weight. I don't miss the heat of his palm against the sliver of skin that is exposed from beneath my shirt and pants.

"So do you," I say as I lean forward, pushing him back against the arm of the couch.

I slide my hand through his hair, watching the color shift in his eyes from gold to copper.

"I can stop, if you want me to," I say as I lean in.

His gaze falls to my lips, his fingers digging into my hip.

"I just... need you to know that we don't *have* to do anything if you don't want to," I assure him, though I'm not sure if I say the words for his sake, or for my own.

I just know that I want him, more than I've wanted *anyone,* and I don't want to fuck this up.

There is a heavy silence as he shifts his position, sinking back as he brings his legs up on both sides of my body, forcing me to fall further between his legs. His cock twitches against my stomach and he gazes down at me.

"That's the thing that's scary," he says, chewing his bottom lip. His gaze darkens. "I don't want you to stop."

I slide my hand beneath his shirt, feeling his warm skin, those pronounced hip bones that cut below his waistband. I run my fingers over the outline of his cross slowly, relishing in the way my touch makes him catch his breath.

"I don't want you to *ever* stop," he says. His left hand finds my hair, and his fingers intertwine in my locks and he pushes just the slightest against my head, his cock twitching against me. His breath is shaky and for a moment, I think he's going to wake up and realize what's happening. That he's going to freak out and leave me here, hard and wanting again.

"Tell me what you want from me," I say softly.

Geo's fingers grip my hair tightly. "Everything," he says.

I hook my fingers into the side of his shorts, tugging at them as his fiery gaze settles on me.

"Everything, huh?" I breathe, pulling down his shorts until they are around his ankles. I look up at him: his pupils blown, teeth sunk into his lower lip, skin flushed, long lashes standing out beneath his glasses.

I settle my hand over his prominent bulge, noting he fills up my hand pretty well. I grip him softly, if only because I want to ease him into my touch. I want to take my time, because I want this to be good for him. I want the experience to feel *right*.

He sucks in a breath as my thumb presses against the head of his cock through his boxer briefs and he curses breathlessly.

So fucking perfect.

I want everything, too.

Everything he is willing to give me.

I've never felt like this about anyone else.

Just him.

And I think it will *always* be him.

"Are you okay?" I ask, lazily tracing lines against his cockhead.

"Yes," he says, blowing out a breath. "I just need—"

"A minute?" I ask, a smirk forming on my face.

He shakes his head. "No. More. I need... more."

He tightens his grip in my hair, pushing me once more, this time with a little more force, but it isn't startling or uncomfortable. His fingers tremble in my hair slightly, and I know what he needs.

I hook my fingers into the waistband of his briefs and pull them down slowly, watching his expression as I do so.

His amber eyes are like a five alarm fire, ravaging my soul.

I shift my focus, taking in the sight of his bare cock on display before me.

It falls back against his stomach, pink and swollen with irrefutable desire, his precum glistening in the light that pours through the windows.

Just like the rest of him, it's absolutely perfect.

"Tell me what you need, sunshine," I say as I slide my hand along his shaft, committing the velveteen hardness to memory. I hold him in my fist, but I don't move, giving him a chance to answer me.

"I—" His cheeks flush, and he focuses his

gaze on me. For a moment, I think he's going to tell me to stop, but instead he licks his perfect mouth and says, "I want you to make me come."

My own cock weeps at his words, and I let out a curse of my own under my breath.

I build a steady rhythm with my fist, slowly and leisurely. I watch as every pump, every swipe of my thumb across his wet slit makes his face contort into an expression of pure desire.

"Does that feel good?" I ask, feeling his cock twitch in my hands.

Geo nods furiously. "Fuck, yes."

I grin, because I know what's coming, but he doesn't.

His fingers tighten their grip in my hair.

I love how responsive he is to just my fucking touch.

I swipe my tongue along his shaft, and he nearly jumps off the couch.

"Too much?" I ask. His grip in my hair tightens like a vice.

"No. Not enough," he says, his voice all tight and raspy.

"Tell me what you want, baby," I croon as I give him another lick. The salty sweetness of him dissolves on my tongue, and I do it again, expecting a reaction, but he doesn't jump this time. Instead, he relaxes, thrusting his cock up against my tongue. I know what he wants, but I want him to say it.

I want him to *own* his pleasure.

"And don't be polite about it, either," I tease.

His gaze catches mine, full of fire and heat.

"I want you to stop teasing me and put my cock in your mouth and make me fucking come." He blows out a breath, taking his bottom lip in between his teeth. "Please," he says, flashing me with a smirk, a glimmer of that sweetness dancing in his eyes, and I don't waste a second.

I take him into my mouth, into the back of my throat in one fell swoop, and he grips my hair so tight, I think I'm going to have a tension headache for a week.

"Oh my God." His voice strains as he thrusts himself into my mouth.

I'll show you God, Geo Graves.

I roll my tongue around his head, cupping his balls with my free hand, letting my fingers tease and massage them.

"Oh fuck," he curses as I lave at the saltiness of his precum.

"I'm coming," he cries, with more cursing

like a damn sailor. "Fuck, I'm coming!" His voice rises as he holds my head with a vice-like grip as he fills my mouth.

I look up at him, seeing the absolute *bliss* all over his face. I take my time leaving his cock, swallowing him down. When I move to wipe my mouth, Geo only pulls me closer, crushing his mouth against mine.

His rough, hungry kiss makes my cock throb, and when he slides his tongue in my mouth, groaning, I think there is no going back from this.

His hands settle at my waistband as he kisses me messily, his hand finding my aching cock.

"What about you?" he asks, his voice thick with lust.

"Don't worry about me." I press my lips to his.

"I want to make you feel like... this..." He sighs against me.

"Like what?" I ask, slowly grinding my cock against his palm.

"Like Heaven," he says, and I think I'm well beyond the point of salvation.

I'm no longer hell *bound.* I've set up a fucking villa in Hell.

I gaze into his eyes, and the spark in my chest becomes a wildfire.

"You already do, Geo," I reply as I kiss him slowly once more, savoring the feel of his perfect lips.

"You are *Heaven Sent*."

CHAPTER 21

Geo

THERE IS no escaping family dinner. Especially because Katy and my parents know exactly where Zeb lives.

He'd offered to host the dinner tonight, I think, because he knows I'm already on edge around my mother. But I'm not sure what's worse—being around my mother and the white picket fence shit, or having my parents sit on the couch my former bandmate slash boyfriend-ish person just sucked my dick on while said boyfriend-ish person currently cooks dinner five feet away.

When my phone rings, I thank God for the intervention.

"It's Mateo, I'm just going to... uh... yeah, I'll be back," I utter as Katy raises an eyebrow suspiciously.

She clutches her wine glass, standing next to Zeb as she glares at me.

It's weird, I won't lie. For starters, my sister is all of five foot three and one hundred and twenty pounds soaking wet, and Zeb is like a grizzly bear next to her, but the way she's looking at me is like *she's* the Mama Bear out to get me.

When I get into the guest room, I shut the door.

"What's up?"

Mateo's smooth voice sounds in my ear.

"My sister has commandeered me and my boyfriend to join her and Richie on a trip tomorrow to the Grand Canyon."

I don't miss the sarcasm in his voice.

"Oh, a road trip, how cute," I tease him.

"It's a two hour drive from the hotel," he bites.

"You don't sound particularly thrilled. What's wrong?"

"Did you hear me? I'm going to spend two

hours in a car with the Wylde brothers and my sister, and you're asking me what's wrong?"

I laugh.

"You sound bubbly as fuck. Things going well with the new demographic, I take it?"

I can't help the smile that forms on my face, knowing no one can see me.

"He has a name, you know."

"Really, I wasn't aware," he taunts me.

I shake my head. "His name is Zeb."

Mateo pauses dramatically. "Your former band mate?"

There is no surprise or shock. I find his lack of a reaction, refreshing.

"You should bring him." His tone is serious, and it's not a question.

Panic, shame, and guilt threaten to build up again. I bite my lip.

Like a... date?

"Geo?" Mateo calls, pulling my attention.

"I mean, I guess we could come, but I'll have to run it by him first."

Mateo purrs on the other end of the phone. "Excellent. We're heading out around ten, so we can all meet up around noon in the parking lot. Hailee's booked us a private tour."

Right, of course. Hailee and Mateo have always been pretty high profile, but with their young, rising-star boyfriends, I doubt they'd be able to just join a regular tour.

All of them, especially the *Heart Killer* boys, are not easily disguised.

At least if I want to disappear, all I have to do is take out my contacts, dress in preppy clothes and a ball cap, and I'm good.

Zeb knocks on the door, opening it just slightly. "Everything okay?" he asks, and my heart skips a beat.

God, he is so beautiful, and I feel my entire body relax at just the mere sight of him.

"See you tomorrow, Geo," Mateo says, then the line goes dead.

"Uh, yeah," I say chewing my lip as I think about Mateo's request.

Zeb looks behind him, then slips into the room, shutting the door. "You look like you've seen a ghost," he says as he reaches out, running his fingers along my hip.

In my peripheral vision I can see us both in the mirror, standing there.

I can see the way his larger frame engulfs me,

and the memory of his fucking head between my legs resurfaces.

"Would you want to go to the Grand Canyon with me? Tomorrow?" I ask. "You know, since the concert was postponed and all…"

Zeb smirks, running his fingers along the skin beneath my shirt. The touch is soothing, warm.

"Like a date?" he asks, his tone so much more confident than mine.

"I mean, there would be other people there…" I say, licking my lips. "Mateo, his boyfriend, Dare. Hailee, her boyfriend Richie."

"Ah. Your label mates," he states.

"My friends," I reply, hoping he understands. Mateo and Hailee are like family to me.

And while I don't know the Wylde brothers that well, I know that Dare and Richie are young, bright, and fun and a hell of a closer to Zeb's age than I am.

I think it might not be such a bad idea. Maybe… maybe it would work out okay?

"So you want me to meet your friends?" he asks, his voice even. Deep, dark.

I nod. "Yes."

He pulls me closer. "You still owe me for the Gardens," he says darkly.

I brace myself, my hands on his hips. Heat engulfs me from the way he looks at me.

No one has ever looked at me the way he does.

"I do not. I—"

He smirks. "Now you want me to meet your friends." He shakes his head. "Are you always this demanding, Geo Graves?" he whispers against my ear, his breath hot on my neck, his sweet and tempting scent all I want to breathe.

I bristle in his hold, my cock standing at attention.

"Maybe," I admit.

His hand slides over my ass, and I tense immediately, looking at the door and I freeze. He slips it beneath my waistband, his palm hot against my flesh. A mad blush forms on my cheeks, heating me like a flame.

"Seriously?" My voice lifts, high-pitched.

"You can tell me to stop," he says with the sexiest grin I've ever seen on anyone. Man or woman.

"My parents and sister are out there..." I mumble, flustered.

"How bad do you want me to meet your friends?" he teases, slipping his fingers right over my seam.

I suck in a breath, trying to breathe as my cock twitches. "What about dinner?" I ask, heat ransacking my body. "What about my fucking parents?"

"Your dad is manning the grill in the backyard, and Katy and your mom are on their second glass of wine."

I look up into his eyes, knowing I'm going straight to hell for what I say next. I rest my hand on his cock, my palm heated.

"Really bad," I declare, gazing up at him.

He leans down and kisses me, and I feel like the world falls away.

"How bad do you want me to suck your cock right now?" I ask.

Zeb raises an eyebrow at me, smiling deliciously.

"Really fucking bad." He clears his throat. "But only if that's what *you* want."

I glance at the door, then back at him, sin blooming in my core.

I've spent my entire life being *good*. Even when I left and started my career at Casualty, I was still perpetuating my "Good Christian Values" by wearing my ring.

I twist my fingers over the steel that I haven't taken off in sixteen years. The heat from my skin warms it, as I realize my boundaries aren't defined by anyone else.

Not by my mother, or Kevin, or the label, or even the public.

It's up to me.

It's a *choice.*

I slide my ring off my finger and set it down on the dresser.

Zeb grins.

"Yes. I want it." I say, signing my death certificate.

God can't save me now.

I slide up to Zeb, focusing on his gaze as I pop the button on his jeans, and I take a deep breath, sliding my hand inside his boxers. His cock is warm against my skin, thick as I hold him.

I push him down with one hand and he falls against the foot of the bed, looking up at me with dark, lust-hazy green eyes. I take in the sight of him like this—arms braced on the messy bed, his thick cock bouncing freely—and I half worry I might actually choke.

God, that would be embarrassing as fuck.

But despite the fear, the worry, and the panic, I want this.

I want *him*.

"Holy fuck," he says, looking up at me.

"What?" I say, grabbing my cock, if only to adjust myself.

"You look so fucking hot right now," he says, and his voice is barely a whisper.

"Do I, now?" I ask as I take one step forward, then another, until I am between his heavy legs.

Zeb nods as I drop to my knees before him.

I lick my lips, slowly squeezing him at first.

"Time's ticking," he says, but his tone isn't hurried or rushed, or even pushy by any means.

It's warm.

It's safe.

It's home.

I say a silent prayer that I don't die suffocating on his dick, and then I close my eyes and I just do it.

I jump off the fucking cliff and take him into my mouth.

His dick is smooth and salty in my mouth and I don't miss the way he curses under his breath when I do so.

I run my tongue up and down his shaft, sucking his cockhead like a popsicle on the Fourth Of July.

His fingers find my hair, and he slowly thrusts himself into my mouth.

I meet his motions, getting used to the feel of slight suffocation. I can still breathe, and the sensation of the strain only makes it feel better. I want to consume him.

I want *everything.*

I force my mouth down a little farther until he hits the back of my throat. It's uncomfortable, but it doesn't hurt terribly and I don't choke like I thought I would.

Zeb threads his fingers through my hair, gripping tight.

The motion only makes me want more, so I repeat the motion once, then twice. I find a rhythm as I let my tongue slide along his shaft, as his thickness hits my throat.

"You sure you haven't done this before?" he asks, cursing.

I answer him by rolling my tongue around his cockhead like a lollipop. His groan makes my own cock twitch.

"Because fucking hell, Geo, you are killing me right now."

His praise lights me up like a morning in church.

I explore his cock with my tongue, my mouth, and before I know it, I feel him pulse, his cum filling my mouth.

I swallow it before I can think about the fact it's cum.

Not just cum, but *Zeb's cum.*

The taste isn't terrible, if I'm being honest. I kind of like it.

I feel a wide grin spreading across my face because I just made him come.

Guess I'm not so bad at it after all.

I rise, wiping my mouth as Zeb looks up at me with a look that shakes me to my damn core.

"Zeb, where are you?" Katy's voice sounds, and I feel a strange sense of pride as I watch Zeb tuck his cock away, zip his pants, and straighten himself out.

"Coming!" he calls, and I have to stifle a laugh.

When he leans in and kisses me, slipping his tongue into my mouth, I think this is everything I've ever wanted.

"You are going to send me straight to Hell, Geo Graves, you know that?

I smirk. "Thought you didn't believe in Hell, Z."

"That was before you deep-throated my cock on the first shot, sunshine." He gently smacks my ass as he opens the door.

For the first time in my life, I feel like nothing can take this feeling away.

Because for the first time in my life, I know exactly who I am.

AFTER DINNER, I move to clean up the dishes, but Zeb tries to stop me.

My mom smacks his hand away.

"If a man offers to do the dishes, Zeb, you let him!" she teases and he tenses, as Katy gets up to help gather glasses.

"Walk with me," she says under her breath as I clutch the plates to my chest.

I follow her into the kitchen, while my mother and father talk to Zeb, noting through the window that he's blushing.

"What do you think you're doing, Geo?" My sister's voice is solid, unwavering. Serious.

I turn the water on, sudsing up the sink with dish soap. "I don't know what you're talking about," I lie.

"Bullshit. I know *something* happened between you two because I haven't seen Zeb this happy since you two played together."

I tense at her words, glancing at her as I hand her the first dish.

She takes it bitterly.

"Can't two people just... connect again?" I say carefully.

Katy glares at me. "You know he's in love with you, right?" Her words are like knives.

Love?

I look out the window, watching how my mother sets her hand on his arm, how my father animatedly talks, and how Zeb smiles.

"And you "patching shit up" with him, acting like old times... it's not fair to him. It's not fair to lead him on and let him think you have feelings when you—"

"I would never hurt him, Katy."

Her eyes glisten. "Maybe not intentionally," she says softly.

She dries the last dish, flashing her gaze at me.

"But you're not *staying* here, Geo. This—" She motions around the kitchen, "is not your life. It's his. And he worked really fucking hard for it."

Her words settle on me like a steel beam.

"And I don't want to have to put him back together again when you *leave.*"

Her eyes water.

"And you're going to leave, because that's *your* life. Hollywood, world tours, studio recordings, chasing the charts and living the dream *you* worked so hard for."

I don't have the chance to respond before Zeb opens the door, my mother trailing in behind him.

Katy's entire demeanor shifts as he pulls out his phone, showing her something, and she grins happily.

I watch the two of them together, and can't help but feel envious.

She took care of him.

For ten years.

Because I *left.*

My mother slides her arm in mine as she pulls me toward the front porch.

"I'm sorry about earlier, baby," she says softly as I follow her, Katy's laughter echoing in the room.

I turn to see Zeb with his acoustic, and my dad laughs.

We stop on his front porch, the music wafting out from the living room. He's playing another cover. Lady Gaga. Sounds like *Hold My Hand.*

Katy sings along, and Zeb joins in.

"I know," I say softly as I sit on the porch swing.

She settles next to me. "I just want you to be happy, Geo." Her voice is barely a whisper. "That's all I've ever wanted for you."

I lean my arms over my knees, staring at the ground. She makes it sound so simple. Like the ends justify the means.

But they don't.

"Zeb, too, you know," she says carefully.

I turn to look at her. "What?"

"He's a good kid. Shame he's gay, because he would have made an impeccable husband." She sighs. "But I suppose he'll make some deserving *man* very happy someday."

Her words are heavy in the air.

She knows he's gay?

And she's supportive of it?

She rocks us back and forth.

"It's not that simple mom." I sigh.

"You took your ring off." She runs her fingers over the empty spot.

Shit, I'd forgot to put it back on.

"Just forgot to put it back on." It's not a complete lie. I look away from her, ready for the judgment, but it doesn't come.

She turns my face to look at her, and the look in her eyes is so full of love it's hard not to react.

"It has always been a choice, baby," she says softly. "It was never meant to be a punishment."

I run my fingers over the barren spot. "It felt like punishment," I declare softly.

The memories of my youth, of my father's talk, of all the fights about my girlfriends, staying out past curfew, the chaperones at events... all of it comes back and lodges a knot in my stomach.

She holds me close. "We all make mistakes, baby."

I see the tears in her eyes, and I don't have it in me to be angry at her. I know I need to forgive her, and I need to forgive myself, too.

"Whoever it is, I hope they know you are a

gift," she says. Her words are shaky, and I realize all at once, perhaps she isn't as oblivious as she appears.

But that doesn't mean I'm going to open myself up to her all the way.

I know the path to forgiveness starts here, but I'm not ready to be *that* vulnerable. I haven't even had any champagne.

"Whoever?" I ask.

She nods, a tear falling down her cheek. "Yeah, baby. Whoever." She gives me a soft smile.

And as we watch the Arizona sunset from my whoever's porch, her hand squeezing mine, I feel the warmth spreading over my skin, that bare spot no longer cold.

I can't help but appreciate the sight, as Zeb's rich voice carries in the air with Katy's, singing about holding someone's hand and never letting go.

When she gets up from the porch and heads into the house, I don't move. Not until after my parents and my sister pile into their SUV, until the streetlights come on.

CHAPTER 22

Zeb

I run my hands through my hair, relishing in the steam of the shower. I barely register the door opening, but I don't think much of it. Having to share a bathroom sucks in general, but I'm sure there are plenty of *Gravedigger* fans who would pay good money to share a bathroom with the hottest man on the planet.

I note his silhouette in front of the sink, and I think he must be "putting his face on" as he calls it. I swear, he's got more makeup and hair products than Katy and all her girlfriends combined.

I just toss some fucking gel in my hair and call it a day, but Geo's got *serums.*

Whatever the fuck that is.

I close my eyes, letting the water run over me, and then the shower curtain opens. His dark eyes implore me, and my gaze travels down his tattoo to realize... he's completely naked.

And I finally see the end of his tattoo.

Just above his fucking dick.

My breath catches in my throat as he steps into the shower, his dark gaze confident as hell.

Anyone who says this man isn't sexy has to be fucking blind.

"What are you doing?" I ask, a smile forming on my lips.

"I just figured we both need to shower, and this will save a lot of time." He grins as I set my fingers on his hip.

"Show me yours," he says seductively, reaching for my shampoo.

"Oh, is that what we're doing?" I ask, running my hands through his hair, working up a lather. He lets me tilt his head back, and the sight of the water and soap running down his pale skin, down the line work of his cross tattoo, is a fucking sight.

"That is absolutely what we're doing," he confirms as he leans up and kisses me. "Please."

This fucking man.

I shift in the small shower, turning around and showing him my ass. His fingers graze over the outline of the tail.

"*Hellbound*," he says softly, his fingers hot against my flesh. They slide over my hip once more, and he pulls me back against him. His cock throbs against me, his hands sliding across my barely-there four pack, fingers splayed as the slip through my coarse hair.

"My favorite," he breathes, his lips warm against my skin.

We kiss and touch until the shower runs cold.

Geo heads for his guestroom, towel around his waist, and I don't hesitate to follow as we laugh, tease, and sing along to my blaring blue tooth speaker, like fucking teenagers.

And when we crash onto his bed, tangled limbs and cocks, and hungry lips, I think there's nothing more perfect than this. Than feeling his heartbeat beneath my palm, his precum painting wet trails against my stomach. His fingers gripping my chest hair or grazing my thick facial hair while we kiss like they do in the movies.

I can't keep my hands off of him, and he doesn't seem to mind one fucking bit. Because he can't keep his hands off me, either.

I make him come twice before we leave, only relenting when neither of us can ignore our growling stomachs or the inevitable traffic if we leave too late.

We barely make it out of the house on time, too caught up in one another to remember a world outside us exists.

I watch him in my truck, singing along to Taking Back Sunday's *Make Damn Sure.* His dark hair blowing in the window, his glasses catching a glare.

He sings, tapping along the rhythm against the side of my car door.

I can't resist singing along with him.

I can't resist *him.*

We pull into the parking lot of a place I don't recognize for lunch, but the place looks interesting enough, and we're both starving.

I open his door and he jumps down, sliding his hands in his blue jean pockets. His pale skin doesn't look so pale anymore, and I can see the faint beginnings of a tan.

He catches me staring, looking at me over his glasses. "What?"

"Nothing," I reply. "Just appreciating the view."

Geo rolls his eyes as we head for a table, but stops when someone *screams* his name.

I watch his face fall, and he turns. A woman with an excited expression stands with a group of friends, all of them with their phones ready.

"Oh my God, it *is* him! It's *Gravedigger*!"

Geo flashes me a pained expression.

"Can we please get a picture?" one friend asks while the other waves a sharpie.

"Ohhh, can you sign my boob? Pretty please?"

Geo bites his lip, nodding. "Yeah, of course."

I watch as his entire demeanor changes. He takes off his glasses, handing them to me, runs a hand through his hair, shakes his head, and his spine straightens. He extends his arms, the muscles fully on display and the girls curl into him easily as he strikes a pose.

He smiles, shaking their hands, signing their tits, and I'm reminded just who he *actually* is.

He's a famous rockstar who's performing in just a couple days.

And then he's going to leave.

My stomach feels sick because I don't want him to leave. Not again.

I want him to stay.

Here, with me.

I shove the pain down, because I know if I let it, it will consume me.

What are you doing, Zeb?

"Sorry about that," he says, putting his glasses back on.

"Mateo said Hailee booked a private tour, so we won't have to worry about... that on the hike."

I nod, my mouth going dry. "Of course."

Geo talks animatedly about his friends as we wait for our food, about the new songs he's working on, even though he doesn't have an album put together yet. He's waiting to see how the tour does, if the label will greenlight a new album.

And the whole time, all I can think about is that history is repeating itself.

Just like Katy warned me it would.

"You okay? You seem kinda quiet," he says as he throws down his credit card.

"I told you I was buying," I say.

Geo dismisses me with a wave. "I am not letting you get away with paying for my ass this entire week, Zeb. Seriously. Let me buy you a fucking meal."

His words shouldn't piss me off, but they do. Or maybe I'm just pissed because I let myself fall.

I let myself fall into Geo's open grave, and now I'm buried six feet under.

Fuck.

"Fine," I snap.

"Are you sure you're okay?" he asks. He signs the receipt, sliding his card back in his wallet.

"Peachy," I mutter as I try to shove down the demons threatening to bleed onto everything.

Geo raises an eyebrow, but he doesn't push. He checks his phone.

"Mateo said they just got there. They'll wait for us."

"How nice of them," I gripe, forcing a smile.

I turn the music up, but Geo doesn't sing. He just watches out the window as the landscape blurs.

The beginning notes of Dashboard Confessional's *Stolen* graces the air as we pull into the private parking lot Mateo sent directions for.

Geo climbs out of the car before I can open the door.

And then I see them.

The Starr's and the Wylde's.

Mage Of Mercy and two halves of *Heart Killer*.

"Hey G!" Hailee squeals as she runs up to hug him.

Richie slaps him on the back.

Dare grabs his shoulders.

But Mateo is looking right at me like a fucking asshole.

Geo turns, motioning for me to come over, and it takes everything in me to force the smile, because I feel like I'm falling apart.

I feel like we're going to fall apart.

"Hi! I'm Dare!" Dare chirps with the enthusiasm of a monkey on cocaine.

"Nice to meet you, Dare." I respond, trying to be polite.

"This is my boyfriend, Matty—"

Mateo roves his gaze over me. "It's Mateo," he says cooly.

Mateo is tall, dark, and commanding. His aura is off putting. It's not warm and friendly like Dare or Hailee. It's serious, like he's a CIA agent or something.

Hailee, who is much prettier in person than she is in photos, rolls her eyes, pulling me in for a hug that I can barely respond to before Geo tugs at my hand.

"Don't mind him, he's harmless," she whispers in my ear.

"This is Zebulon, my—" His voice trails off, and when he looks at me I die a hundred deaths.

"Friend," I say, my heart breaking on the word.

Because that's what we are, right?

We were friends, once.

Then he left.

Then he came back, and we were friends, but we are also... more.

But I also know that this thing between us isn't clearly defined, and I haven't wanted to push it because I don't want to push *him* into something he isn't ready for.

But not being able to call him my fucking boyfriend is a new sort of pain I never thought I would experience.

It dredges up all my fucking insecurities, all my demons.

Because that's all I can be, right?

A friend?

Because he's *Gravedigger.*

He's a two-time grammy winner who tours the world and writes sexy songs, and reaps my fucking soul from a world away.

He's a rockstar, and he's going to *leave.*

He's going to leave *me* again.

I don't miss the way the sparkle in his eyes dims.

Because of me.

I am the worst boyfriend-not boyfriend ever.

Mateo extends his hand. "It's always a pleasure to meet someone Geo holds in such high regard."

His grip on my hand is like a vice.

I squeeze back, using my own strength. "Who did you say you were again?" I bite.

Dare chuckles. "I like this demographic."

"What?" I ask, dropping my hand as Geo pushes me away, his cheeks scarlet.

"Okay, that's enough meet and greets for the day," he says and his friends laugh.

Am I supposed to know what that means?

Great, now I'm out of my fucking element even more.

Thankfully, the hike takes most of our concentration.

Geo's arm brushes mine, warm and sweaty, but he doesn't say anything.

When we finally get to the spot we've been hiking over an hour for, Dare drops, groaning about how hot it is, and how hungry he is.

I watch as Mateo finds his way over to his boyfriend, pulling out some snacks and drinks, and I can feel Geo's gaze burning a hole in my back.

"What's your problem?" he asks, his tone bitter.

"I don't know what you're talking about," I retort as I slide my hands in my pockets. I know we're all a bit tired, sweaty.

"You've been a dick ever since lunch. Did I say something, do something?"

I let out a breath, feeling like even more of an asshole.

"Is it because I wouldn't let you buy lunch, because—"

"No," I interject.

"Then why are you acting like this?"

"Like what?" I snap.

"Like someone I don't know."

I look at him, arms crossed over his chest.

"I just don't think your friends like me very much," I reply, noting the way Mateo is watching us. "Especially Mateo."

Jealousy prickles all over me, and I can't help it. He's pretty high profile, and he's been linked to some very high profile dudes, including that actor that just won Sexiest Man Alive or something.

He's a fucking *rockstar* and he's been texting for days, and he and Geo are *close*. And now he's ten feet away, watching us.

Watching *him*.

"I think he likes you," I mutter, looking away.

Geo's eyebrows shoot up. "Are you fucking serious? He has a boyfriend!" I don't miss the surprise in his voice.

I shrug, watching as Mateo turns to his *boyfriend*.

"Dude's been staring at you all fucking afternoon, G. And he's been texting you all week."

I watch Geo's eyebrows narrow. He looks *pissed*.

"Are you fucking blind? He's had his tongue down Dare's throat for the last five minutes." He scoffs. "And he's my *friend*." He crosses his arms, the motion drawing attention to the definition of his muscles, the pronounced veins. His dark eyes burn.

"And, you know, my *friend* who I was really excited to bring on this fucking double triple fucking date bullshit today is being a dick. So yeah, I'm sure he's judging the fuck out of you right now. I am, too."

"Geo…" I suck in a breath, feeling like the world around me is actually disintegrating.

Mateo makes his way over to us, Dare still parked on the ground.

"Everything okay?" Mateo asks.

Geo glares at me. "Peachy."

"We're ready to head back if you are," Mateo says.

Geo grins, but it's not genuine. "Yeah, sure."

Geo says nothing to me the entire hike back to the parking lot. Instead, he sidles up next to Mateo and Dare. Which only pisses me off more, and when we get to the parking lot, I make a beeline for my truck. He walks past me, toward the large black SUV Mateo is standing in front of.

"Hey, where are you going?" I call.

Geo turns to look at me with eyes of fury as he piles into the car next to Dare. "Out with my actual *friends.*"

So this is how I die a second time.

CHAPTER 23

GEO

I POUR myself another glass of champagne as Felix raises an eyebrow.

"You know you don't have to run through your missed teenage years in five days, right, Geo?" His tone is clipped.

Duncan settles next to him, setting down a plate of nachos.

I shoot him a glare as the blur starts to set in. "I'm taking a page of my sister's book," I say petulantly. "Apparently she drinks when the men in her life fuck her over."

Felix raises both his eyebrows as Mateo grabs the flute from my hand.

"Hey, I was drinking that," I whine.

"You aren't going to find the answer to your problem at the bottom of your glass, Geo. Trust me."

Dare climbs into Mateo's lap again, and I have to look away.

Mateo shoves him off.

"What's wrong?" Dare slumps down next to me.

"Everything," I bite as I grab the bottle of champagne.

Felix takes it off of me.

"Jesus Christ Geo, it can't be *that* bad."

I rub the bare spot of my finger, and Felix curses under his breath.

"Oh, shit. You took the ring off."

My bleary eyes meet Felix's cerulean gaze. "I forgot to put it back on," I say, but even I don't believe myself.

"What ring?" Dare asks, but no one answers him.

"Go home, Geo," Mateo says, wrapping his arm around Dare.

"I don't know where home is anymore," I

say, feeling the weight of the world on my shoulders.

How did things get so complicated?

Mateo catches my gaze, but it's Felix who speaks.

"Home is with your *boyfriend*, idiot." Then he gripes, "Sorry, I meant your *demographic.*"

"He called me his *friend*," I say. My gaze falls. "I don't want to be his friend."

Dare rubs my shoulder. "Then tell him that." He chews his bottom lip. "Men are stupid. Sometimes they need it spelled out." I watch him smirk at Mateo.

"What if—"

"Your ride is here," Mateo says smoothly.

What ride?

"I'll walk you out." He climbs to his feet, and I follow, confused.

"I didn't ask for a ride…"

Mateo stops in front of a black SUV. "I know," he says warmly. "But Dare's right. Don't tell him I said that, though."

I sigh. "I think I love him, Matty."

Mateo doesn't correct my drunken slip up like he does with everyone else, and for that I'm thankful.

It only highlights how drunk I actually am.

He opens the door for me. He smiles. "Then tell *him*, not me." And then he shuts the door.

WHEN I GET to Zeb's driveway, I am terrified.

That I'm going to walk through his door and he's going to be pissed at me.

I slide my hands in my pockets, hoping he's still awake, since I know it's late. If not, then I'm going to have to go to my parents' for the night.

And showing up on my mom's doorstep, half-drunk at one in the morning is probably not good idea no matter how old I am.

Plus, I'm sure Katy would kill me. There's no way she wouldn't put two and two together, even if Zeb didn't call her.

I'm surprised when I push the door and it opens. The lights are dim, and I shut the door quietly. Locking it.

Maybe he's already asleep, and I can just—

"You came back." His voice is deep, dark, gravelly.

And definitely drunk.

"Of course, I came back," I reply, toeing my

shoes off at the door. I walk slowly across the tile, noting where he sits on the couch, shirtless. The low lights cast a golden glow on his skin, shadows dancing and making his dark hair thicker across his chest, alongside his jaw.

His green eyes are dark, sad, and I stand in front of him for a moment.

My fingers fidget from the habit, turning an invisible ring.

"I fucked up," he slurs, taking a drink of green liquid.

I see the Sour Apple Pucker on the coffee table, about half full.

And then I see the jar of maraschino cherries, several little stems lined up on a napkin, tied into knots.

"Zeb—"

He stands, and the motion draws my attention to his massive frame and height. He towers over me, his eyes glistening with sadness.

"I let you down," he says softly, burying his face in my hair.

I fall into his warmth, my hands tightening their grip on his hips.

"Fuck, the first chance you gave me to step up…" He runs his hand over his weary face.

"I shouldn't have put you on the spot like that," I state, feeling my own sense of guilt. "I just…"

He glances down at me with watery eyes.

"I'm sorry," he cries.

He fucking *cries.*

"Can you forgive me?" His voice shakes, and I come undone.

I wrap my arms around him, nodding my head as my own tears stain my cheeks.

"It's okay," I assure him, my own voice shaking. "You're okay. Of course, I forgive you." Tears are coming to my eyes like rain as I bury my face in his chest, the thick hair tickling my jaw.

I let his intoxicating scent fill my lungs, let his warmth envelope me. Regret swells inside of me, for words never said, actions never taken.

I made a choice all those years ago, and that choice cost me everything I held dear to me.

My family, my best friend.

I don't want history to repeat itself.

Maybe it's the alcohol, or maybe it's the mid-life crisis taking hold since my birthday is only three days away. But whatever it is, I don't fight it.

Because it feels *right.*

"I love you," I whisper, and the silence is deafening. I slide my hand over his pecs, feeling his heartbeat beneath my palm.

His hand grabs mine where it lays.

"Zeb, I—"

"I have always loved you," he says as he squeezes my hand, his lips finding mine, and he tastes like cherries and sin, like heaven and hell.

His kiss burns through me like an eternal flame.

He grabs my face in his hands, his fingers sliding along my neck and into my hair.

Everything is a blur as the heat of our truth takes hold. His hands pull at my shirt, I pull him by the waistband of his boxers, and we crash into chairs, bump the counter, and nearly take out the framed artwork in the hall as he opens his mouth, sliding his tongue into mine in languid, messy strokes.

I run my hands over his body, afraid if I can't feel him beneath my fingers that he's going to slip right through them.

I slide both my hands beneath the waistband of his boxers and I shove them down, freeing his perfect cock.

His fingers fumble with the button on my

jeans and we both hobble around, knocking into walls and doors as our mouths and tongues fight for dominance as we shed our clothes like snakeskin, needing to evolve.

To become something new.

Zeb breaks away for a moment, staring down at me.

His hand slides between us, his fingers stroking me, the pad of his thumb collecting the fresh blossom of precum that's already gathered at my tip.

I let my head fall back as the haze of alcohol and sex forms a fog around me.

His lips assault my neck as he takes both of us in his hand. The feel of his bare cock against my own, combined with the way his mouth works its way down my throat, makes me see stars.

"Make it up to me," I breathe, finding his mouth once more.

I kiss him hard, slipping my tongue into his mouth, my fingers grabbing his neck.

I push him on to the bed, falling with him like a shooting star.

He looks up at me with glassy green eyes, his fingers sliding into my hair, and I straddle his thighs. The edges of my vision are hazy, but he's clear. Sharp focus fuels me as I grind myself against his entrance, taking his cock in my hands. His fingers grip the dark sheets.

His lips part as he thrusts himself up against me, and the sound that escapes his chest is like an earthquake, shattering me to pieces.

I've never wanted anyone like this.

I've never wanted anyone like I want *him*.

"Fuck, Geo..." His voice is thick and hazy, and I can barely *think* straight.

I glide my hands over his warm, solid form, and the moonlight shines through his window, casting us in an angelic glow.

"Zebulon," I purr as I lower myself, grinding my wet cock against him. I'm so hard it fucking *hurts*.

Zeb arches his back, his cock sliding against my abs, leaving trails of precum along my cross outline. My cock rests against his smooth opening, and my heart beats in my chest like a freight train.

"Is this what you want?" I ask, pressing myself against him, spreading my precum along his entrance.

Zeb sinks his fingernails into my shoulders as

he leans upward, finding my mouth once again as he kisses me furiously.

"Yes," he growls.

I thrust myself forward, meeting his resistance, but he melts underneath me like a puddle. I keep my gaze fixed on his face, on the way his jaw goes slack, the way his eyebrows furrow.

Zeb curses as he thrusts his cock up against me, seeking friction.

I wrap my hand around his thickness, my rhythm slow as I watch his face contort into one of pure *pleasure.* I thrust myself against him, but it's not enough.

His hand slides between us, and I look down to see him *fucking* himself on his damn fingers, his gaze hazy and dark.

Before I can say anything, do anything, he removes them and I know exactly what I need to do.

I line up myself easily, inching the head of my cock into the space that's a little wider now.

"Harder," he breathes, his voice deep and gravelly, tinged with lust, drink, and love.

I push myself against him, finally breaching him. The tightness around my cockhead makes me see stars and I curse as his mouth finds mine and I sink my own nails into his skin. I pull my hips back, and then I push. Harder. Faster.

Within two distinct thrusts, I bottom out, groaning in his mouth.

God, he is perfect.

Zeb's breaths are heavy and his grip falters between agonizing and wonderful as his arms wrap around me, hands sliding over my ass, up my spine.

"Fuck, Geo..." His breathing is labored and I'm glad I'm not the only one who can't fucking breathe.

My hips move of their own accord, and I relish in the feel of how tight he is, how full I feel. How each thrust becomes smoother with each roll of my hips.

Inside of him, I feel *everything*.

"Promise me," he breathes, his lips trailing kisses over my throat, up my neck.

"I promise," I say, not even giving a shit what he wants to ask for. I'll promise him the world if it means I get to come home to *this*.

My orgasm hits out of nowhere, and I can feel the warmth as my cock pulses, throbbing at the same time I feel him erupting against my stomach.

I look down at him, face flushed, eyes all hazy and pupils blown, lips swollen from kissing me. I kiss him with all that I am. I feel like I could die here, like this.

Buried in the man I love.

The person I know was meant to be mine.

I collapse against him, his grip on me loosening as I slide out of him, as exhaustion takes hold, and I roll over on the bed, my eyes falling shut.

The pillows welcome me, and Zeb pulls me close, burying his face in my neck and hair.

"I love you, too, Geo."

CHAPTER 24

ZEB

MY HEAD IS POUNDING and my body feels more than a little sore.

I open my eyes, slivers of dawn creeping in through my window. My body is warm like a fire. I grip Geo's waist, pulling him closer. The moment he brushes against me, backing his bare ass against me, I freeze.

Panic floods me as I slide one hand between my legs, feeling the evidence dried on the inside of my thighs.

Oh, no.

No, no, no, this wasn't supposed to happen like this...

Geo turns in my arms, rubbing his eyes.

"Fuck, my head is killing me," he groans, as I fight to steady my breath. He squints, looking at me with those warm, amber eyes, and I feel like an even bigger asshole.

"Geo, I'm sorry. I—"

"What are you apologizing for now?" he groans. "I thought we did the apologizing thing already." He slides his arm over my hip, pulling me closer.

"We—" I struggle with what to say because I can barely process what's happened.

We fucked.

Geo is no longer a virgin, because of *me*.

Shit.

Shit, shit, shit.

I can't take something like that back.

Ever.

This is *not* how I wanted this to happen.

"Last night..." I try to wrack my brain for words, but I can't find the right ones.

"Last night was amazing," he says, burrowing closer to me. His hand squeezes my back.

I freeze again.

"We were drunk," I say, as I wrap my arms around him, hoping to hold onto this moment a little longer before he really leaves.

"Yeah, and?" He groans as he threads his leg through mine.

My jaw tenses. "Yeah, and?"

"You don't regret it, do you?" he asks, and I can see the fear striking his face. "Shit, you do, don't you?" Panic floods his face, and I squeeze him tighter.

"I—" I have to think about my words, because I know my answer will make or break more than just us. "No, I just... I don't want *you* to regret it," I say.

Sunlight streams through the window.

Geo purses his lips as he touches my lips with his fingers.

"I don't," he says softly.

I part my lips just the slightest as he grazes his thumb over my bottom lip, and the way he's looking at me soothes my fucking soul.

He kisses me, and all the tension, all the anger, all the pain, disappears.

In that kiss, I feel *everything*.

"I waited thirty-nine fucking years, Zeb. Let

me have this, okay?" he says, his voice dark and full of humor.

"I feel like I've corrupted you somehow," I say, with a laugh of my own.

"You did," he says, holding me close. "But now I know what make up sex feels like, and I can totally see the appeal now."

His phone rings out from down the hall, and I look at him as he traces his fingertips along my beard, and I realize I need to shave.

"You going to get that?" I ask.

Geo rolls himself over top of me, pressing me into the mattress with a smirk, planting another soft, feathery kiss on my lips. "Nope."

He settles his weight against me, but the position isn't overtly sexual.

It's comforting.

I trail my fingertips along his ass, up his spine.

My body aches, knowing where he's been, and my heart aches knowing where he's going.

The phone rings again.

And again.

"You should probably answer," I say as he groans, rolling his eyes.

When he shifts off of me, I feel the emptiness of his weight.

I throw myself out of bed, heading for my bathroom to get showered. Being covered in dried cum is not as appealing as it sounds.

When I get out of the shower, I find Geo across the hall in the guest bedroom, packing up his guitar.

"What's up?" I ask, leaning in the doorframe.

"I'm late for sound check."

Sound check, right. The show...

The show's tomorrow.

And so is his birthday.

Tomorrow, he's going to be forty.

Originally, Katy and I had planned to take him out for dinner, then follow up at his parent's house for cake and ice cream, but after dinner the other night, and the postponed show... Katy and I haven't really discussed alternate plans.

And I'm not entirely sure she isn't pissed at me right now because I called her last night crying that I'd fucked up.

I do have to give her props for not telling me "I told you so," but something tells me if she finds out what *really* happened last night...

Yeah, I might disappear in the desert somewhere and become an urban legend.

"You guys are coming to the show tomorrow, right? I mean, your tickets should be honored since it wasn't a full cancellation, but if they give you shit, Kevin—"

"Yeah, of course," I reply, watching him sling his guitar case over his shoulder.

"I'll drive you," I offer as he shakes his head.

"No need, Kevin sent an Uber."

Who the fuck is Kevin?

Anxiety and panic start to cycle again, and Geo must notice. He steps up to me, placing his hand on my stomach.

"Kevin's my manager," he says softly. "He's just doing his job."

"Right," I say.

His fingers slide over my hip, drawing lazy circles. "What?"

"I just hate to watch you leave, that's all," I utter, feeling more naked than I did when I woke up with Geo's dried spend all over me.

Geo settles his free hand around my neck, pulling me lightly against him. My forehead rests against his.

"I don't *want* to leave," he says, his voice barely a whisper.

"So don't leave," I implore his gaze with my own.

Pick me.

Choose me...

My heart beats so loud I think he can surely hear it.

Geo purses his lips, his fingers sliding into my hair. "It's not that simple, Zeb. But for the record, I wish it was," he says, as I hear a car pull up.

"See you later?" he says, stopping in front of my door.

I take a moment, committing him to memory, like this.

Guitar slung over his shoulder, dark hair a little mussed, thick glasses framing his face, dressed in tight black jeans, a faded white shirt, and a leather jacket. A glimmer of youth marred with the shimmer of the present.

I look at half my heart, standing there in the living room, and I want to fall apart. But I can't.

I have to be stronger now than I was then.

"Yeah, of course." I force a smile, if only for him.

Because as he walks out of my house, jumping into a sleek, fancy car, I know that my time with him is limited.

Because perfect things don't last *forever*.

CHAPTER 25

Geo

"You sounded great up there!" Kevin pats me on the back as he heads backstage.

I sigh, knowing I should feel excitement and happiness because I *did* sound really good. Better than I have at the last few shows, even I know that.

But despite sounding good, I don't *feel* good.

In fact, I feel like shit.

I know I can't blame my mood entirely on the alcohol, though.

"Thanks," I reply as I slide my hands in my

pockets, taking a look at the empty stadium before me.

I take in the sight of the rows and rows of seats that go so far back, they look like they'll disappear into the night sky when it's dark.

The place is filled with noise right now, but it's an ambient sort of noise.

Wheels of carts scratching on concrete, echoes of stagehands chattering, and faint melodies in the distance as assistants, managers, and musicians all scramble about to make sure everything is set up right, that everything is in its right place.

I suck in a deep breath as I look at the empty seats beneath the stadium lights, knowing that tomorrow this place will be full of thousands of people.

It's a bittersweet thing, the calm before a big show.

"Hey..." Mateo's voice pulls me from my thoughts and I realize I'm the only one still out here on the stage. *Heart Killer*'s good and gone.

"Hey," I answer as he slowly ambles over to me.

"I noticed you were a little pitchy during that last verse in *Heaven Sent*," he says calmly.

He stands next to me, hands in his leather pants.

I purse my lips.

"And you looked a little lost when you were singing *Devil In Me*."

"Yeah, I guess I'm a little distracted. Rough night." I shrug. It's not entirely untrue.

"Mhmm," he murmurs as he takes a seat on the edge of the stage.

The sleek, long black walkway jets out into the center of the pit, and though right now it looks like nothing more than an empty concrete circle, tomorrow I know it will be filled with screaming, moshing fans.

I take a seat next to him, staring up at the empty stadium, soaking it all in.

This is my life.

This is what I always wanted.

Isn't it?

"You ever think about what your life would be like if you weren't Mateo Starr?" I ask, turning to look at him.

Mateo's gray-blue eyes implore mine. "No," he says firmly. "I mean, I always knew this was it for me. Hailee, too. Music was our salvation, you know."

I nod. "Is it everything you wanted?" I ask, folding my hands in my lap. I settle my gaze on some stadium workers sweeping between the floor seats stage right.

Mateo sighs. The grin on his face is heavenly. "No, it's better." He nudges my arm, pulling my attention. "It's not, for you, I take it?" He says the words plainly, but they are heavy on my heart.

I glance at my hands in my lap, at the bare spot on my finger, noticing my absent-minded fidgeting.

"Maybe it was, but I'm not really sure it is anymore," I admit.

Mateo's voice softens. "What do you want, Geo?"

I think about his question, but the words I want to say are stuck in my throat.

"I don't know," I reply, watching the lighting crew plug in and unplug wires, spreading them across the floor, getting ready for Mateo's sound check.

"Yes, you do."

"Mateo..."

"You've always known *exactly* what you wanted. Ever since the day you signed with Casualty, and I suspect you knew before you left being Geo Graves."

I look at him as my chest tightens.

"This…" He motions around the stadium. "It doesn't *feel* right for you. It never has. Because you never wanted to do this alone. It didn't feel right doing it *without him*."

I wring my hands together as the knot forms in my stomach.

"You've just never said it *out loud*," he says.

"Maybe, but it's still my life," I state, gazing out at the empty seats. "I chose it."

Mateo's voice is smooth, serious. "This life isn't for everyone, you know. A lot of people never make it to the other side." He looks at me with the same kindness he did all those years ago when I was the new kid on the label. When I was a twenty-nine year old, blond, boy next door who had no idea what he was doing, or how he was going to do it.

He could have been an asshole to me, but he wasn't. He took me under his wing, and he helped me become *Gravedigger*, and I will always thank God for his guidance and friendship.

"I know." My voice is tinged with melancholy.

"But you don't have to stay, you know," he breathes the words with sincerity.

I turn to look at him, my eyes widening. "What?"

Mateo's eyebrows furrow. "Your heart hasn't been in this for awhile, Geo. We both know that."

I want to respond, to say no, he's wrong, but...

He's not.

Mateo is a lot of things, and an astute observer is one of them.

"Passion is what inspires people like us, Geo. Not sales numbers and *demographics,*" he says, flashing me with a smirk.

"You, me, Felix... even fucking Dare..." He huffs, but I don't miss the way his lips smile when he says his boyfriend's name. "We all need to *feel* that passion, that spark. Not just in the *music*, but in our fucking soul."

I settle my palms on the black stage floor, my fingers leaving prints on the acrylic.

"Yeah." I nod, rubbing my hands along the smooth, chilled surface. "I get it."

I can feel the tears threatening to form in my eyes.

I feel it, the spark.

The passion.

But I don't feel it *here*, in this stadium.

I don't feel it in LA in my too big house, or even in the recording studio, anymore.

"No, I don't think you do," he retorts, shaking his head. "You can stop, Geo."

I have to close my eyes to try and hold off the fucking tears that want to free themselves from my soul from his words.

"It doesn't have to be *forever*. You can take a fucking break." He sighs. "Look at Drew. He went home to Jasper Springs and fell in love, took a hiatus. I left for five years and came back and released *Satellites* and went on this fucking tour. Met the goddamn love of my life, too. And look at Duncan—he *had* a big career, left, got married, had a kid—came back and look at him now. Dude is *killing* it with the rest of us and his pain in the ass boyfriend, what? Twenty, thirty years later?"

His words settle on me, and I look up at the clouds, the light that pours through them onto us from above.

The tears fall because I can't fight them.

"You wouldn't be the first guy to take a

break, and you certainly wouldn't be the first guy to take a break because he fell in love."

I look up at the sky, and the clouds have parted.

Mateo squeezes my shoulder with warmth.

I want to respond, but all that comes out of my damn mouth is a sob. I pinch the bridge of my nose as I sit with my friend and the truth.

The truth I've known, but I didn't want to admit.

The truth of what I *know* I need to do.

For my heart, my sanity, and the sake of my *music.* But most all, for me.

God didn't give me a second chance to make the same mistake twice.

"Three months," I say softly. I look at Mateo's familiar face. "Three months left on this tour, and then that's it." My voice is a little more solid as I let the truth settle, as I find my strength. "Yeah, I think a hiatus is long overdue."

Mateo offers me a kind gaze, squeezing my shoulder once more. "I'm going to miss having you around, Geo Graves."

I settle my hand over his, offering him a genuine smile. "I'm going to miss having you around, too, Mateo," I swallow harshly. "Thank you."

Mateo drops his hand. "Of course. It's not goodbye forever."

"Mateo!" Hailee calls out. "Are you ready or what?"

We both turn to see her at the back of the stage with her keyboard, and suddenly, I get an idea.

"Hold your fucking horses, Hailee!" Mateo snaps as he stands, offering me his hand.

I take it and he helps me to stand. "It's just goodbye for now," I say as I exit stage left.

ZEB

THE HOT ARIZONA air kisses my skin, a stark contrast to the chill from my A/C as I open my sliding glass door.

Katy is putting the final touches on the back patio with balloons and streamers while Joel sets up the grill.

Twenty-four hours.

Somehow a week has fizzled down to mere hours, and the truth is bittersweet.

I know the show is tomorrow, and Sunday morning, Geo will jump on his tour bus, and he'll be gone, and when the tour is over, he'll go home to L.A. and it'll only be a matter of time before the next album comes out, and the next tour starts.

Because that's *his* life, but it could have been mine, too.

So, I'm not going to waste the precious time I have left with him before he leaves.

After Geo left for sound check, I called Katy. If twenty-four hours is all I have left, I want to make it the best twenty-four hours.

I never got to see his thirtieth.

I want thirty-nine to go out with a fucking bang.

But most of all, I need him to know how much I fucking love him.

"Zeb, baby, where do you want me to put this cake?" Debbie calls me from inside, pulling me from my thoughts.

I head back indoors, my gaze settling on the petite blonde woman in my kitchen, holding a giant cake box.

"I got it, Mrs. Graves," I respond. I move to grab it off of her, our fingers brushing.

She crosses her arms, shooting me a suspicious look. Her bracelets clink and clang as she looks around the room.

"What?"

"You did a beautiful job," she says, as I set the cake on the island.

I reach for the cake stand in my upper cabinet, the one I never use. The only reason I even have a cake stand is because Katy brought it once for a picnic and she keeps forgetting to grab it every time she visits.

One glance at all the decorations that Katy and I put up, and I have to admit, my house kind of looks like Party City threw up in here, but somehow, it is perfect.

"I can't take full credit. Katy—"

"I'm not talking about the party, Zebulon," she declares.

I set the cake stand down, heading for my silverware to hunt for a cake server, or at the very least, a big fucking knife.

I stop in my tracks as she comes to stand next to me as I open the drawer.

"Mrs. Graves—"

She goes right in, pulling out a server as she flashes me a sly grin. Her long, manicured nails tickle the back of my hand and she looks at me with glistening eyes.

"I know things haven't been easy for you. I

know this..." She sighs. "This didn't come easy, either. But you never *gave up,* Zeb."

Her hand squeezes mine, and I feel a sense of pride mixed with validation I never knew I needed.

"So don't give up now." She smiles softly.

I wallow harshly as her words fall on me. "I—"

She removes her hand from mine. "Don't give up when it's just getting good, baby." She winks at me, just as Katy opens the door, her heels clicking on the tile as she fusses with the champagne bottle.

"Zeb! I need a big strong man to open this fucking—" She blushes for a moment, looking at her mother. "Sorry, Mom."

Debbie sighs. "Not my house. Not my rules." She smirks at me as I take the bottle from Katy, popping the cork with a loud bang, her words still heavy in the air.

Is she... saying what I *think* she is saying?

I don't have time to process her words, as fizzy bubbles spew out the top as Geo walks through the door, and time stands still.

"What the—"

"Happy Birthday, baby!" Debbie says as she holds her arms out.

Geo looks from her to me to Katy, and I don't miss the way his eyes sparkle or his lips twist into a grin.

"What is all of this?" he asks as she hugs him tight, letting him go only so he can breathe, I think.

Katy takes the bottle from my hand and pours the champagne.

Geo slowly walks across my kitchen, stopping at the island, leaving a modicum of space between us.

"I should have told you, I absolutely can *not* drink this stuff," he says with a smirk.

"Oh, don't be so dramatic, Geo. Champagne is for celebrating." She waves his off dismissively as she reaches for a glass.

"Hold up," I say as I head for the fridge, pulling out the perfect touch.

I unscrew the lid of maraschino cherries and set them on the counter, plopping four into one flute before I push it to him with a grin.

"You are all terrible influences." Geo smiles, and it makes my heart skip a beat as he takes my offering, shaking his head.

Katy lights the candles on the cake as Joel comes inside.

I slide a little closer to Geo, close enough that our arms touch. It's a subtle touch, barely perceptible in this space with his parents, but it's enough to draw his fiery gaze to mine.

"Happy Birthday," I sing, and everyone joins in.

"Make a wish," Katy says with a grin.

Geo slips his arm around my shoulders, the fire of the candles dancing in his amber eyes.

He closes them, blowing the candles out, and everyone cheers.

IT'S NEARING ten-thirty when everyone finally leaves.

Geo strums away on my acoustic, perched on my couch.

I swallow harshly as I approach him, my heart in my throat, knowing what I'm about to do.

I settle next to him and he stops, fiery amber eyes staring up at me.

I reach for my guitar and he lets me take it.

"Any requests?" I ask.

Geo twists his lips, tapping his finger against it. "Hmmm, let's see…" He pretends to think, but I have a feeling I know what he's going to pick. "*Hellbound*," he says, softly. "If you still remember it, that is."

I grin. "Of course I remember it. I wrote it for you."

Geo's eyebrows furrow as the truth falls on him.

I strum out the first few chords, watching his face.

"I swear it's destiny, I swear it's fate
You're all I want, but everything I can't take
I don't want to fight this, but I have to stand my ground
But baby, don't you know I'm a sinner
And you've got me Hellbound."

Geo's gaze falls to my hands where I play, and then he sings.

"Heaven won't take me because I'm a sinner
Earth won't keep me on the ground
My heart wants to fly beyond its cage
I want to scream but I can't make a sound
Because every time you look at me, baby, I know I'm Hellbound."

I hadn't expected *him* to remember the words.

Or to sing them to me.

My heart wants to leap out of my chest, and I layer my voice with his.

"On my knees I beg, I wish, I pray
That one day you'll see you're lost
And one day I'll be found
I'll wait here forever for my angel
Because I'm forever Hellbound."

I close my eyes, his hand on my thigh squeezing tight as he sings the last chorus right along with me.

I strum out those last few chords, the soft melody fading into the warm golden twinkling lights around us.

My gaze settles on him as I rise, holding out my hand.

Geo takes it without question, and I lead him down the hall to my bedroom, where his gift is.

After he left this morning, I knew exactly what I needed to do.

And I'd be lying if I said I'm not nervous about what his reaction will be.

"Stay here," I say as I take a moment to grab the small bag.

When I turn around, he's standing against my dresser, hands in his pockets.

"You didn't have to get me anything," he says. "Really."

I hand him the small bag and he takes it.

"I know. But I wanted to."

I needed to do this, not just for him, but for myself, too.

I watch as he pulls out the small box, opening it. And then I watch his smile fall over his perfect mouth.

"Do you like it?" I ask, running a hand through my hair nervously.

Geo stares at the velvet box, as I casually pluck it from his hands, taking out the smooth, black tungsten ring sitting inside. A tangible promise he could feel on his skin, a reminder of my promise that I'd be here when he is ready to come back. When he's ready to come *home.*

"Thought you could use an upgrade," I murmur, and he smiles. He doesn't fight me when I take his hand and slide it on.

He sets the box on my dresser as he slides his hand on my hip.

"I love it," he says softly as he leans into my space.

I fall into him as the faint whispers of Secondhand Serenade sing like angels from my linked bluetooth speakers.

There is so much I want to say, so much I want to tell him. I'd been running over exactly the right words all day in my head, but somehow they all disappear the moment I look at him.

Well, all except *three*.

"I love you," I whisper to him, wrapping my arms around his waist, holding on tight.

He wraps his arms around my neck, our bodies nonchalantly moving to the beat, pressed together.

The fire in my heart catches everywhere.

Geo kisses me with reverence as his fingers delicately work their magic over the buttons of my shirt.

I slide my fingers in his hair, relishing in the soft feel of it against my fingertips.

I let him undress me, let him take his time.

Because I want to savor this moment, too.

The moment before everything perfect disappears.

I spin him around so his back is flush against me as I work at the buttons of his jeans, sliding them and his briefs down.

He removes his shirt with haste.

I trail my lips over his neck as I pull him against me, his bare ass brushing against my cock as I wrap my arms around him, one hand splayed across his chest, while the other holds his cock in my hands. When I look up, I can see us in the mirror, can see him staring at our reflection, and I think there is no better sight than him like this.

Than *us*, like this.

He slides his hand over my right hand across his chest, his shiny new promise ring glinting in the light.

I watch his eyelashes flutter, his heartbeat racing beneath my palm.

He pushes himself against my twitching cock.

"Tell me what you want, birthday boy," I whisper in his ear.

"You," he breathes, reaching his hand back to slide his fingers through my hair. His voice shakes slightly, his grip on my hair soft and reverent.

I thrust myself against him without a second thought, relishing in the little sounds he makes, the way his heart skips a beat when I do so.

"I want to feel *you*," he breathes, his voice strained. "Everywhere."

"Are you sure?" I ask. I lazily stroke his cock, his precum warm as it slides along my palm and his shaft.

Geo nods against me, and I feel him beneath me, his legs parting just the slightest as he leans forward. He looks at me over his shoulder.

"I'm sure."

I remove my hand from his chest only to open the drawer to grab the lube, my heart in my throat.

My stomach flips with a hundred emotions.

I've never done *this* with anyone. I've never *wanted* to.

I've always been more than comfortable to be the person who takes whatever someone else feels I deserve.

I've never been the person to *give*.

But I want to give him everything, even if all I have to give is me.

My heart.

The liquid is cool against my skin, sending a shiver racing through me, but Geo doesn't even wince.

He braces his hands on the edge of my dresser, closing his eyes as I slowly slide my fingers along his seam, into his tightness.

I go slow, letting him get used to the sensation, taking in the sounds of his pleasure as I do so. With one hand, I use two fingers to slowly stretch him, while I stroke his cock with my other hand.

His gaze catches mine in the mirror, and I know I'll remember this moment forever.

The calm before the storm.

"If it's too much, just tell me, okay?" I plant a kiss on his shoulder.

Geo nods as I line myself up.

I slide into him slowly, but easily, and my entire body locks up the moment I bottom out.

Geo finds my hand over his cock, leaning his head back against my shoulder as he pushes back against me and my body reacts of its own accord. For a moment, I can't even move, too consumed by the feel of him wrapped around my cock.

I let out a low groan and Geo slowly pushes back against me.

I pull my hips back, relishing in the feel of the drag. I thrust myself into him, the movement easier, smoother this time, and he lets out a heavy sigh, his hand squeezing mine.

Tears threaten to escape me as I try to get a

handle on the emotion that is so familiar, yet so new as the truth lands in my brain.

So this is what making love feels like.

The soft acoustic melodies of Dashboard Confessional's *Heart Beat Here* is like a choir of truth as I let my lips trail over Geo's skin, as I let myself feel all of it, all of him. His heartbeat beneath my palm, his precum against my fingertips, his sweet orange blossom and cedar scent, his soft, breathy moans, his tongue in my mouth. I savor the sounds he makes, the way he responds to my touch, the steady beating of his heart.

His cock pulses in my grasp, filling my hand with warmth as I empty myself inside of him.

"Happy Birthday, baby," I whisper in his ear, glancing at our reflection.

When we finally separate, we find our way to my bed wordlessly.

Geo curls against me as I drape an arm over his hip, pulling him closer until all I can breathe is him.

And only then do I fall asleep, praying that the morning never comes.

CHAPTER 27

GEO

"So, when you get there, Kevin—"

"Yes, yes, I know, we've been over this." Katy rolls her eyes. "You're going to be late if you don't get going."

Kevin throws my luggage and my guitar in the trunk of the SUV.

"She's right, you know," he says, deadpan.

In just eight hours, I'll be taking the stage as *Gravedigger*, and I'll be making the news official.

After this tour, I'm going on a hiatus. I've already spoken to Kevin and the label about it.

After my heart to heart with Mateo, I knew exactly what I needed to do.

And after last night, I know now more than ever, that it's the *right* thing to do because it's what I want.

Because Zeb is what I want.

Kevin wasn't expecting such an announcement, and as such, the label was quick to respond to his important call. Though, to their credit, no one seemed to crazy over the whole "*Gravedigger* is in love with a guy" thing, but I guess the label's had their hands full with gay awakenings and announcements as of late.

Something in the water, indeed.

Though they understood, more than I thought they would, and assured me that when I was ready to return to the studio, ready to return to being *Gravedigger*, I could. I'm sure my lack of sales and discussion of a new record were an easy out for them, too, even if they didn't say anything.

I know I can never stop making music, regardless, because the music is a part of my soul, but it's only part of the equation.

I'm made up of more than just black hair dye and contacts, after all.

Of course, I haven't told my family or Zeb yet. But I plan to. Tell them, that is.

Along with thirty thousand other people tonight when I take the stage with the help of my friends.

Kevin approaches us, and I hear the door shut.

I turn to see Zeb standing on his porch, thick tanned arms drawing my attention from beneath his rolled up sleeves. My gaze settles on his messy dark hair, his bright green gaze. The sliver of dark chest hair sticking out from beneath his plum collar.

Once I stood in front of him, my heart in my throat as I made the hardest decision of my life, ten years ago.

I don't regret leaving in the sense that I know now, I needed to do it. I needed to learn who I was, I needed to experience the world outside of my bubble.

I needed to become *Gravedigger* so I could understand who Geo Graves *is*.

And now I know.

I know exactly who I am.

"Okay, G, we really do have to head out if we want to beat traffic," Kevin warns.

I nod. "Yeah, I know," I say as Zeb slowly saunters down the steps.

Katy pulls me into her arms, her grip tight. "I'm going to miss you, asshole," she says softly in my ear. "Don't wait ten years to come back next time, okay?" I can hear the sadness in her voice.

I tighten my grip on her, her auburn hair tickling my face.

"I won't," I say, knowing my sister and I are going to have a lot of time to make up for.

And that's also something I'm looking forward to, too. Even if it does involve sour apple martinis.

When she lets me go, I turn to face Zeb.

His hands are in his pockets, and the sky opens up with the brightest light behind him.

"Break a leg, sunshine," he says, pulling me into a hug.

I can't help the way I hold onto him. I clutch him close, breathing in his sweet tonka-bean teakwood scent. His scratchy beard brushes against my face, and I press my lips to his.

In front of my sister and my manager.

Zeb startles, but only for a moment as he relaxes and takes my face in his hands.

When we break apart, I smile, turning to Kevin, who's got wide eyes.

"See you guys later," I say as I head for the car.

I watch through the tinted windows as we pull out of Zeb's driveway, watch as my sister comes to stand beside him, watch as they both wave goodbye.

"You ready, G?" Kevin asks, making sure my mic pack is secure.

The lights dim, and I know this is it.

"Ready as ever," I say as the lights completely go out.

In my earpiece I hear the countdown.

Ten. I take a deep breath, shaking out my limbs, loosening up.

Seven. I crack my neck, closing my eyes as I focus on the sound of the fans screaming, filling the air.

Five. I clear my mind, focusing on my heartbeat.

Two. I open my eyes as I step out into the darkness, my boots clicking across the stage until

I find my spot in the center. Richie's bass echoes around me as Dare's guitar shreds through the air, Spike grazing his cymbals as the keys of Hailee's synth keyboard echoes with the beginning notes of Real Life's *Send Me An Angel*.

And then the lights open up, bathing me in neon blue light.

I look out at the sea of people, but there's only one face I really want to see.

I ask the crowd if they believe in heaven and they roar as the band behind me plays, and I take a moment to soak it all in.

When I ask if they believe in love, the cheers sound like heavy rain.

So do I.

The lights are bright and they drown everything out as I strum out the chords along with my backup band.

The spark in me ignites, fueling me like never before as I feel the lyrics in the depth of my soul.

I scream-sing the lyrics, begging to be sent an angel right now and they cheer like mad.

I saunter up the landing where I sat only a day prior, looking out into the vast crowd, searching for my angel.

And then I see him.

Stage right, arm in arm with my sister, next to mom and dad.

I can't help but grin when I see him, dressed in black jeans, his dark hair styled over his face like he used to wear when he was younger, sporting a *The Used* shirt. Gold glitter rests along his cheekbones, and the black eyeliner rimming his green eyes makes them stand out all the more.

Slivers of the young man I once knew flicker with the man who stole my heart as he smirks at me.

Katy jumps up and down, grinning from ear to ear, sporting the same gold glitter across her face and in her hair.

My mom watches me as I grab my microphone, taking my stance, the same way I always do, and I don't miss the look of pride on her face. Or my father's.

The sight is most... validating, if I'm being honest.

I can feel the heat of the pyrotechnics behind me as I grip my microphone tight and I do the one thing I've always done when the world around me feels too much.

I sing.

I sing my fucking heart out, because for the first time since I left all those years ago, I feel it.

The spark.

I take a moment to find my breath as I finish the song, take a moment to really appreciate all that God has given me.

Dare's guitar rolls us right into *Devil In Me*, and I don't miss a beat.

I prance around the stage like I fucking own it, because tonight I do.

I own it *all*.

I sing every song from the depths of my soul, unafraid of what I know is coming.

Finally, we hit the last song, which is normally *Heaven Sent*, but I decided to change things up a bit for this show.

What kind of rockstar boyfriend would I be if I didn't serenade the man I love in front of thirty thousand people?

The band quiets, and the crowd is thunderous.

I put my finger to my lips. "Shhhhh," I tell them as Kevin pushes the piano out for Hailee.

I stand there, sweaty, hot, and grinning.

"You know, yesterday was my fortieth birthday," I say and the crowd cheers. I can't help but laugh.

"And I gotta tell you all, it made me think about a lot of things."

A stage hand pushes a stool out for me to sit.

I run my thumb over my lip, wiping away the sweat.

"Show of hands, how many of you knew me before I was *Gravedigger*? Who here knows who *Geo Graves* is?"

There are more cheers than I expect, and I smile as I drop my gaze to stage right.

Zeb smirks.

"Well, for those of you who don't know, I used to perform music a lot different than what I do now. And it only feels right, that here, in my home, in the place that built me, I pay a little tribute to my Christian Rock days as Geo Graves. That is, if it's okay with all of you?"

Their cheers are infectious.

"Oh, thank you so much guys! I truly appreciate it. Can I ask you another favor?"

My heart thuds so loudly in my chest, I think it's roaring with the crowd.

"Could you pretty please light up the sky for me? Get those phones and lighters out?"

I watch as the darkness fills with bright, teaming light, and I think God really does work in mysterious ways.

"Thanks, guys. You're the best," I call out as I ready my mic, looking at Hailee.

The beginning keys of Philip Wickham's *It's Always Been You* graces the air.

I sing, my voice shaking, as those first few words find their way into the darkness, the truth in them so profound.

He did see me first, after all.

Hailee's haunting piano playing mixes with the sway of the lights, and I close my eyes and feel the music.

Feel the truth.

I clutch my chest, if only to keep my heart from leaping out as I sing Philip's evident words, about God being there for him in the past, and being there for him in the future. But it's not God I'm serenading tonight, though I am more than thankful for this moment he's pushed me toward.

I open my eyes, pausing as the tears form in my eyes as I sing about all the years *his* love was breaking through the cracks. The clarity of understanding is cathartic as Mateo's words meld with my truth.

I've always known what I wanted.

I just never said it out loud, but I am now.

I sing from the bottom of my fucking heart, that it's always been *him*.

It's always been Zeb, from the start.

I step down from my stool, walking slowly down the landing to stage right as I sing about castles crumbling and being pulled out of the fire, out of the water.

I sing about being *saved.*

And when I reach the end of that landing, I fall to my goddamned knees in front of him, and I sing.

His bright green eyes glisten, and in them, I can see the truth so clear.

He gazes at me like I'm not on a stage in front a stadium full of people. He looks at me, and I know he sees *me,* Geo Graves.

He sees my soul, and there is nothing greater than that.

The crowd around us fades into shadows and lights.

It's always been him, and it'll always be him.

When I stand, I take slow steps back to center stage, and I stand in the center of it all, and I smile. I belt out those last few lines, and then they cheer.

"Shhhh..." I wave my hand, motioning for them to be quiet, and they listen.

"You know, music has always been my passion, and nothing is ever going to change that," I say, licking my lips.

I sigh, letting out my truth for the first time. I find him, my strength, and the words come naturally.

"This is going to be my last tour. For a while," I declare, my shoulders relaxing as the crowd quiets.

"I will always be grateful, for you. Every single one of you. I promise it's not goodbye forever, guys. It's just goodbye for now."

It's quiet for a moment before the crowd erupts into sounds of happiness, of support, of love.

I smile at Zeb as the lights dim, my cue to leave.

"Good night, Tucson," I shout as I exit stage left to find Mateo with Dare in his arms, his eyes teary-eyed.

"That was fucking beautiful, man!" Dare cries through a sniffle.

"So romantic," Hailee says as she comes up next to us. "Thanks for letting me be a part of it."

I smile at them, nodding in approval, heading for the dressing room, if only because the nerves have finally hit and I need a minute to process it all.

I find my reflection in the mirror, eyes red-rimmed, cheeks flushed with heat and sweat, my hair a mess, and I take a moment to feel the spark. I know it'll keep me warm, always.

That safe, warm spark that makes me feel *alive.*

And then I see the door open, and familiar green eyes meet mine in the mirror.

CHAPTER 28

Zeb

It's impossible to not feel the star power of Geo Graves in a room of thirty thousand screaming fans.

Even when we played for crowds of one hundred, he'd always had this way of connecting with an audience. Making the performance feel personal, even though it was more or less part of his job. His act.

He was always magnetic, warm, and inspiring, but watching him perform *It's Always Been You* was an out of body experience.

Watching him fall to his knees, hand clutched to his chest, hearing the *power* in his voice, the *love*...

And then he looks at me.

In a sea of people, he looks at *me.*

And then he stands up, saunters his perfectly fine ass across the stage, and I can barely breathe.

Katy tugs at my hand, pulling me out of a tear-filled stupor.

"Must've been some kiss," she whisper shouts in my ear. She looks up at me with watery eyes, the glitter on her face lighting up from her smile.

Debbie pulls my attention from her daughter.

I wipe my wet eyes, noticing hers are teary, too.

We all are.

She reaches out, her fingers smoothing my vintage tee.

"He's quite a gift, isn't he?" she says, biting her lip.

"Yeah, he is," I respond as she smoothes her fingertips over my frayed collar. Her nails tickle my neck as she sighs.

"And all this time, I thought it was going to be Katy." She laughs.

Katy laughs, too, and I can't help but cry and laugh, too.

Joel hugs his daughter, shaking his head.

"What are you still doing here? Go! He's waiting for you!" he orders, and I don't have to be told twice.

I make my way through the crowd, heading for the side of the stage.

I flash my VIP pass, but the security guard doesn't seem to buy it.

"He's with me," a deep voice echoes, and I look up to see the ominous Mateo Starr, decked out in black leather, hands slipped into his pockets with that stoic steely gaze. He steps out from the shadows, nodding at the security guard.

"Of course, Mr. Starr," the guard replies, and Mateo nods for me to follow him.

We stop just behind the stage, and I know he's going to have to go on soon, and I need to find my boyfriend—

"I'm only going to say this once, so listen close, Zebulon."

I stare him down as he lets out a deep breath.

"Be good to him. He's one of the fucking good ones."

Before I can say anything, he holds his hand up.

"If you break his heart, I will come for you."

His threat is not without levity. The way Mateo Starr speaks, I totally believe he'd kill me.

And something about that is comforting. Like a big brother protecting their younger sibling, and I think I understand now.

He took care of Geo for ten years. He was a source of comfort and friendship, and all at once, I feel thankful for the lumbering man in front of me.

"Noted." I offer him my hand. "Thanks."

He shakes it, his grip firm.

"Room seventeen," he says, dropping his hand. He slides his lanyard off and hands it to me.

I hold it in my hand, understanding befalling me. My lips twist into a grin.

"Thanks, Matty."

Mateo growls, flipping me off as he turns around. "It's Mateo to you!"

When I find room seventeen, I have to take a

deep breath of my own. My heart races, my pulse heated as I slide the card and open the door.

Geo stands in the center of the room, staring at his reflection in the mirror. His gaze captures mine, and I shut the door, the mechanism whirring to tell me it's locked.

It's just us.

Now, and forever.

I walk up to him slowly and he makes no point to move.

"You were amazing up there," I tell him as I lean in and kiss him. I can taste his sweat and tears on his lips, and it's a sweetness I never thought I'd know.

"You really think so?" he asks, innocently, as if he has no idea how powerful he is.

How utterly *perfect* he is.

He's a fucking miracle.

"Yeah, baby," I reply as I run my hands through his hair.

"How'd you get back here?" He leans his forehead against mine.

"Mateo let me in." I smile.

I don't miss the way his lips turn up into a grin.

"Oh, so you two have had your coming to Jesus moment?"

"Something like that." I kiss him again.

"Are we good now?" he asks softly. "I mean, I know I owed you for the Gardens, and then meeting my friends, and taking advantage of you —" His sarcasm is as sweet as it is sexy.

I kiss him with all that I am. His lips move against mine slowly, and he opens his mouth, letting me in to caress his smooth, warm tongue as I hold him close.

"So fucking good," I whisper against his mouth.

His hand slides in my hair, and I can feel the tungsten steel of his birthday promise ring cool against my neck.

When we break apart, he leaves me standing, heading for the fridge. He brings a bottle of champagne out, his grin sexy and wicked.

"Thought you couldn't drink champagne," I tease as he pops the cork.

"Well, technically, we wouldn't even be here had I not had champagne." He shrugs. "Seems appropriate."

"Well, in that case," I respond as he takes a swig.

His dark eyes are full of fire as he passes me the bottle.

"To champagne," I say as I take my swig.

Geo sets his arm around my waist as I clutch the bottle to my chest.

"To champagne," he whispers.

EPILOGUE

Six Months Later...

Geo

"MOVE, so I can get a picture of this fantastic spread, baby," my mother says, shooing me to the side.

"It's just food, mom. You can't eat the picture."

She waves me off. "It's a milestone, we need all the pictures."

"Mom, stop," I whine.

She takes the picture anyway. "You'll thank me one day," she says with a huff as she continues waltzing around my house, taking pictures of everything.

Though to be fair, I guess there is a lot to document since she's never been here before. My dad follows her, rattling on about my movie-screen size television in the downstairs, insisting I never sell this house. But I know one day, when the time is right, we will. For now, though, while we work on our double album, this house works for both of us.

Katy nudges my shoulder.

"What?" I ask.

She reaches up, running her fingers through my hair. "So not used to seeing your natural color," she says with a grin. "Been a long time since I saw *this* Geo."

I can't help the flush that forms on my cheeks from her sweet compliment.

"Happiness looks good on you, though."

I smile, adjusting my glasses as she removes her hand from my locks. Her phone vibrates on the table, and she grabs it.

"He's five minutes away," she says with a grin. "You ready?"

"You didn't give anything away, did you?" I ask.

She shakes her head as she straightens out the bowls of fruit in front of us. "Who? Me? Never."

I shake my head, running my hand through my hair.

She's the only one who knows my big plan, and I can't help but feel a sense of validation as she grins at me.

"Mhmmm," I murmur as the door opens, familiar incessant barking starting up.

My mother is pulled from her photographic documentation and instead, toddles over to sweep up the newest addition to our family; Angel, the ten pound terror.

Who I'd adopted after three glasses of champagne and a very, very persuasive Zeb.

And I'd be lying if I said I didn't love her and her noisy little Yorkie yips, her little tappy-taps as she runs across the tile, or the way she makes both of us laugh with her cute little puppy dog antics.

The house is never quiet anymore.

It's full of music, incessant barking, and love.

So much love.

When he opens the door, my stomach does a little flip. His bright eyes find mine and he shakes his head, smirking. His dark hair frames his face, a welcome accompaniment to the thick beard that highlights his perfect tan and pink lips.

Thirty looks good on him.

"I should have known," he says as Katy throws her arms around him.

Angel yips, twisting in my mother's arms, and he grabs her, shaking his head with a wicked smile. Angel wags her tail, bathing his arms in kisses.

"You sounded way too excited on the phone," he says, shooting Katy a glare.

Katy sips her sour apple martini and smirks at me as I walk across my kitchen, one hand in my pocket, warm against the box I've been carrying around for the last week.

Zeb rubs Angel between the ears.

"This does not look low-key, sunshine," he says, but his voice isn't angry or unhappy.

It's warm, sweet.

"It was either this or Good Morning America," I tease.

Angel twists in his arms, licking the back of my hand.

Zeb rolls his eyes. "Mhmmm." His gaze travels to Katy's drink.

"There's champagne, too." I smile as I grab

Angel and set her down. I need his hands available for what I'm about to do.

"Champagne, huh? You sure that's a good idea?" he teases.

"Well, thirty *is* a big deal," I say. "Definitely deserves the good stuff." I grin. "Some might even say thirty is where it all begins." I smirk as I pull the box out of my pocket. I don't miss the gasp from my mother, or Katy.

"What is—"

"Your gift. Open it," I say, offering it to him.

He takes it, his fingers shaking as he regards me with a suspicious gaze.

Angel throws herself over our feet, her tail smacking my bare feet.

My heart is in my throat as he opens the box. He flashes his verdant gaze at me with a delicious smirk.

"This what I think it is?" His tone is full of pure love, but there is also a touch of humor.

"That depends, what do you *think* it is?" I tease him.

"I think it's a very pretty tungsten ring." His smile lights my heart. "With very, very sparkly stones."

"Do you like it?" I take the box from his

hand, removing the ring from it's velveteen casing.

His smile is everything.

He is my everything.

"Yes," he responds, licking his perfect lips. His voice doesn't shake, and I can't help my own smile.

The levity of his answer is *Heaven Sent*.

"I love it," he says as I grab his hand.

I'm fully aware my parents and my sister are watching us, but I don't care.

Honestly, I hope my mother gets a picture.

"Happy Birthday, baby." I chuckle, and I press my lips to his. When I break away, I can see the genuine excitement, the happiness in his eyes.

"It's always been you," I whisper as I slide the ring on his finger.

His fingers entangle with mine, warm and familiar, safe and perfect.

His promise against mine.

"It'll always be you," he whispers back.

ZEB

. . .

I open the door from the bathroom and find Geo in our bedroom, sitting cross-legged on the bed in nothing but his black boxer briefs, his thick tortoiseshell glasses sliding down his nose, golden blond hair falling across his temple, that big, black cross accenting his perfectly sculpted chest. He is completely lost in thought, pouring over an array of song papers in front of him.

He doesn't hear me, or see me, and for a moment, I just take in the sight of him like this.

My future husband.

So fucking perfect.

"Oh, hey..." He looks up from his spot, cheeks blushing from catching my stare. His gaze dips to the towel around my waist, and I don't know if I'll ever get over these little moments; the ones where he looks at me with such endearment, such *love*.

"Hey," I reply, sauntering in, taking my seat next to him, on my side of the bed.

"Figure out your ideal arrangement yet?" I ask as I shift closer to him.

He looks at me from beneath his glasses. "Not quite. I mean, I like opening with *Hellbound* and the *Heaven Sent* remix, but I feel like we need an intro of some sort, and then there's Saint, and of course, Sinner, and—"

I slide his papers over with one swift motion, and he shakes his head.

"Zeb," he sighs, but it's not annoyed or defeated.

It's soft, warm, and so fucking enticing. I love it when he says my name like *that.*

"Sunshine..." I smirk as I pull him closer, upending him into the back of the bed. Papers scatter, and he just shakes his head as he tugs at my towel.

"These are the masters," he groans, but he makes no move to fight me.

Instead, he sinks back into the comforter, bringing his legs up on both sides of me, his thighs gripping mine as he runs his fingers along my back and over my ass.

I settle on my elbows, poised above him. "We can make more music," I say as I press my mouth to his warm lips.

Geo wraps his arms around my neck, his kiss slow and sweet as he opens his mouth for me.

Somewhere in the house, Angel barks, and I can't help the smile on my face, or the laughter that escapes my throat.

"So much more," he whispers.

I graze my fingers over his hips, sliding my digits up the expanse of his chest, tracing those perfect black lines along his abdomen.

Geo's fingers tighten their grip in my hair as he lets out a soft moan as I palm his cock through his briefs.

"You still owe me for the party," I tease.

"Oh do I, now?" he asks, thrusting himself up against my palm.

"Mhmmm," I murmur, letting my lips appreciate his neck. "I said low-key, and that was *not* low-key in the least."

"You really are the *Devil In Me*, you know that, right?" He moans.

I pull away from his neck, tracing my thumb over his perfect, pouty bottom lip. His golden hair is a mess, his glasses a little crooked, but the glimmer in his eye is unmistakable, as is the smile on his face.

"I know," I say as I kiss him, as I show him just how devilish I can be. The sound of his ecstasy as he comes, the way he says my name, the wistful way in which he tells me he loves me is my favorite song.

When we are both spent, Geo curls closer to

me, resting his head against my chest as he drapes his arm over my waist. I gingerly take his glasses off, setting them on the bedside table.

And as we both watch the LA sunrise from our bed, I know Heaven is real.

Because it's ours.

Thank you for reading Grave Misgivings!
I hope you've enjoyed the Rock His World series.
Who knows, maybe these sweet boys will show
up again someday.

IF YOU ENJOYED THIS BOOK, maybe you'll do me a huge favor and leave a review. Even a few words would mean the world to me, and it also helps other readers find the stories you love.

THANKS!
~Evie Riley

Kissing Danger

Smokejumpers

Hawke

Cyrus

Jase

Gage

Jackson

Xavier

Jasper Springs

Cade

Dawson

Drew

Grayson

Riley

Mitch

From The Edge

Shattered

Runaway

Jaded

Rescue

Hidden

Tormented

Gray Vale Pack

His Fated Mate

His Wounded Warrior

His Healing Heart

FOLLOW EVIE

Facebook Author Page
https://www.facebook.com/AuthorEvieRiley

Blog/Website
https://authoreveriley.blogspot.com/

Goodreads
https://www.goodreads.com/author/show/39018597.
Evie_Riley

Bookbub
https://www.bookbub.com/authors/evie-riley

Instagram
https://www.instagram.com/authorevieriley/

LGBTQ+ Romance Books ARC Team
https://booksprout.co/author/25823/lgbtq-romance-books

Evie Riley is a prolific, neurodivergent author known for her captivating MM romance novels. She has gained a significant following and topped the LGBT+ action and adventure bestseller charts with her series.

Evie's writing style often explores dark and gritty themes where her men must overcome difficult obstacles in their search for love, but she has also ventured into sweeter small-town romances, incorporating tropes like enemies-to-lovers, friends-to-lovers, age-gap, and forced proximity. She is known for crafting engaging romantic suspense novels and has a knack for creating interconnected series worlds that keep readers invested.

Outside of writing, she enjoys spending time at the beach and has a quirky personality, described by her partner as ranging from cute to deadly, depending on her blood-chocolate levels.

Evie spends her nights writing bad boys in love, and her days wrangling the sweet boys she loves.

www.ingramcontent.com/pod-product-compliance
Lightning Source LLC
Chambersburg PA
CBHW061058210726
48294CB00001B/195